Michael

J.L. Arden

Stratus Publishing LLC

Content Note:

This novel is intended for 18+ Mature Audiences only. It contains explicit language, sexual content, and adult situations.

Contents

Chapter 1
Verónica

Verónica lingered in front of the mirror, tilting her head as though searching for a version of herself she might finally recognize. The soft glow of the vanity lights highlighted the sharp lines of her cheekbones and the curve of her lips, painted a shade of rose she rarely wore. She looked elegant, almost glamorous, but she couldn't shake the gnawing thought that it was all costume—fabric and makeup covering a truth she couldn't quite erase. Tonight, of all nights, she wished she could disappear. Thessaly's wedding was supposed to be a celebration, but Verónica carried too many ghosts to feel at ease. Eleven months had passed since she signed her divorce papers, yet the memory of Gregory's betrayal still clung to her like smoke after a fire.

She tried to smooth her dress, but her hands trembled slightly. For eight years, she had been someone's wife. Gregory's wife. His college sweetheart. His safe, steady choice. She had believed in forever, had staked her youth on it. These were her prime years throughout her twenties. And then, without warning, it was gone—shattered by whispered rumors that became proof: his young secretary, bright-eyed, with the confidence Verónica had never mustered. The revelation had hollowed her. It wasn't just the affair. It was the confirmation of every private fear she had carried since girlhood—that she wasn't enough. Gregory never called her beautiful. Never told her she lit up a room, or that he was proud she was his. Instead, there were criticisms left unsaid but etched in silence, the kind that eroded her piece by piece. The memory surfaced uninvited—Gregory's cousin's engagement party—and with it came the familiar ache of disappointment. Verónica had bought a new dress for the occasion, one she had been genuinely excited to wear. She remembered putting it on, slipping into her heels, and standing before the bedroom mirror, taking herself in. The black fabric fell just above her knees, hugging her in a way that felt elegant and confident, accentuating the curves she rarely acknowledged she had. For a moment, she felt beautiful, certain that Gregory would see her the same way.

When she stepped into the living room, ready to leave, she waited for his eyes to light up, for a word of praise or even a smile. Instead, he glanced at her and frowned. "That's what you're wearing?" he asked, his tone flat. "Don't you think it's a little too revealing for a family function?" The words hit her like a physical blow, her chest tightening as if the air had been knocked from her lungs. Before she could respond, he waved it off with a dismissive shrug. "Oh well—you're already dressed, and we're late. Let's go." And just like that, the confidence she had felt moments earlier drained away, leaving her to follow him out the door in silence.

Her friends tried to convince her otherwise. Her mother, her confidants, Thessaly herself—they told her she was radiant, that she deserved more. But this afternoon, staring into that very mirror, all she could hear was Gregory's absence and negativity.

Verónica swallowed and forced herself to breathe, anchoring her emotions before they could betray her. At twenty-nine, she felt an unsettling truth settle into her chest—at times, it seemed as though she had never truly lived at all. Marriage had come too early, before she had explored who she was beyond the role of wife, before she had learned what it felt like to be admired without question or wanted without apology. Gregory was her first and only. And now she was left with the unbearable thought that maybe she had wasted the best years of her life on a man who never truly saw her.

The sound of tires crunching against pavement pulled her back from the spiral. The limo had arrived. Her stomach clenched. For a fleeting moment, she considered pretending to be sick, calling Thessaly with some excuse. But she couldn't—she wouldn't. Thessaly was not only her friend but also one of her anchors through the divorce, someone who had repeatedly reminded her that there was life after Gregory. Backing out now would be a betrayal, not just of her friend, but of the promise she had made to herself to face the world again, no matter how fragile she felt inside.

Verónica had always wished she could be more like Thessaly or Susan—women who seemed born knowing how to live out loud. Thessaly, even back in college, had walked through life as if she belonged in every room she entered. Men always seemed to gravitate toward her, confident men with polished shoes and plans for the future. They wined her, dazzled her, gave her tastes of love that shimmered like crystal under candlelight. Verónica, meanwhile, had been hidden away in Gregory's shadow, watching her friend sparkle from a distance and wondering what it might feel like to be chosen so easily, so effortlessly.

And then there was Susan—the wildfire. To Verónica, it seemed as though Susan never hesitated, never even considered second-guessing herself. She burned through experiences and lovers with a hunger that both terrified and fascinated Verónica. A one-night stand for Susan was as casual as changing clothes. She would come back from nights out with stories that made Verónica blush—reckless, unthinkable things—and always with that mischievous grin. "You only live once, Verónica," she'd tease. "What if you never get another chance?" Verónica used to laugh it off, but secretly she wondered—what would it feel like to let go? To step outside her carefully drawn lines? She had never dared, not even once.

Now, looking back, she wished she had been braver. She wished she had said yes to more. Yet, even in her regret, Susan and Thessaly had never let her feel alone. They had been there through Gregory's betrayal, through the nights she sobbed until her chest ached, through the endless questions of why wasn't I enough? They caught her when she fell apart, and in their own ways, they stitched her back together.

And now, Thessaly had found something lasting. Verónica believed in it—because Thessaly wasn't the type to leap without certainty. Verónica was certain that if her friend was walking down the aisle, it was because she had finally found a man and a choice that felt undeniably right.

Verónica envied her. She had never had that kind of certainty. She had married Gregory not out of conviction, but out of fear—fear of being invisible, fear of never being wanted again. He was the first man who ever seemed to see her, or at least pretended to. She had wrapped her fragile self-esteem around him like ivy, desperate for something to hold onto. But Gregory never truly held her. He never made her feel like she mattered. No romantic dinners. No late-night surprises. No flowers. No moments of worship that said, "You are mine—you are enough." Instead, there was only his cold distance, his quiet criticisms, and her own reflection whispering that maybe he was right. That maybe she had never been enough at all.

Gregory used to whisper promises in the dark, words spun like fairy tales just for her. "Once I make it big, we'll finally enjoy life," he'd murmur against her skin. Verónica had clung to those promises like lifelines, fragile threads binding her to a future that never came. Now, she could only imagine him whispering the same rehearsed vows to his young secretary, weaving the same illusions he once wove for her.

Gathering her clutch, Verónica stepped out of the apartment. The late afternoon air pressed cool against her skin as her heels clicked against the cracked cement. The driver tipped his cap, smiling warmly as he opened the door. "Good evening, Ms." His courtesy only deepened the hollowness in her chest, a reminder that this was all performance, that tonight she was an actress in someone else's joy.

She slid into the waiting limo. Two bridesmaids were already inside, chatting animatedly, their laughter bubbling bright and effortless. It should have been contagious, but it only made her own silence feel sharper. She smiled politely, exchanged the expected pleasantries, then settled back with a posture just a little too composed, the kind one adopts when the armor is invisible but necessary.

How she wished Susan were here. Thessaly was the bride, the source of so much joy, but Susan had always been the one to read Verónica without words. She would have known how to shield her from awkward questions, how to fill the silences before they swallowed her whole. But Susan was half a world away, in Italy, chasing light and fabric through the lens of her camera. And so, Verónica sat alone among the chatter, smoothing the folds of her dress again and again, silently rehearsing the answers she dreaded giving—about Gregory, about the divorce, about why she had come without a date. She prayed the questions wouldn't come, and if they did, that her practiced smile would be enough to hide the rawness still pulsing underneath.

Chapter 2
Michael

Michael usually found weddings long and tedious—an endless parade of small talk with distant relatives and acquaintances who treated the reception like the grandest night of their lives. He had become skilled at dodging such obligations, often slipping out entirely with little more than a polite note and a generous check tucked into a card. But this time, there was no escape. This was his cousin Thessaly's wedding, and his father had made it clear that Michael's absence would not go unnoticed. Although he wasn't especially close to Thessaly and hadn't seen her much since childhood, disappointing his father was never an option.

Michael had invited Olivia to accompany him. She wasn't his girlfriend—he had made that clear more than once—but she had accompanied him to family gatherings before. Olivia moved easily in these settings, charming enough to deflect questions from nosy aunts and watchful uncles. To them, she seemed more than just a friend, which suited Michael perfectly. It made the night easier to navigate.

He lived a life free from attachments, and he liked it that way. At six feet tall, with athletic arms, a defined frame, and a face that turned heads the moment he entered a room, he had little trouble attracting women. They often sighed. There was something almost electric about his presence—the sharp lines of his jaw, the careless sweep of his dark black hair, the confidence in his stride. Yet it was his smile, warm and disarming, that drew people in completely. Women gravitated toward him, often faster than he could send them away.

Michael had no interest in being tied down. His energy went into his business. He was consumed with building his real estate empire, approaching it with the same discipline he applied to everything else in his life. His mornings began in the gym at six, the clang of iron and steady rhythm of his breath fueling him for the day ahead. By seven-thirty, he was at his desk, fully immersed in the grind, rarely leaving before seven. His schedule was relentless, his drive unshakable, his vision uncompromising.

Friday and Saturday nights were his reprieve, when he indulged, stepping away from contracts and deals into the bright pulse of the social world. Rarely did he spend those nights alone. If it wasn't Olivia, it was someone else. There was always someone else.

The morning of the wedding, Olivia woke with stabbing cramps twisting her stomach and a cold sweat running down her temples. She barely had the strength to pick up the phone. When Michael answered, she whispered an apology—she couldn't make it. Her voice cracked with guilt, but Michael took it in stride, his tone warm and steady.

"Don't worry about it," he said. "Rest. I'll go, stay long enough for Dad to be happy, and call you tomorrow. Just take care of yourself."

Relieved yet unsettled, she hung up. Michael moved on with the quiet decisiveness of a man used to adapting without fuss.

By late afternoon, he was dressed and ready, every detail flawless. His Ermenegildo Zegna bespoke suit hugged his frame perfectly, the fabric crisp under the warm light of his room. He studied himself in the mirror, adjusted his tie, and allowed himself the quiet satisfaction of knowing exactly the effect he had on people—especially women. Then he drove to the reception, stepping into the elegant hall where the scent of roses mingled with faint traces of expensive cologne and champagne.

At the seating table, Michael scanned the rows of neatly printed cards until his eyes landed on his name: Table Four. He followed the line of chairs and found his place among the family. His father was there, along with his sister Beverly and her husband, Nick. Beverly—Bev to those who knew her—had carved out her own reputation as a sharp and relentless federal prosecutor in the Southern District of Florida. Beside them sat his brother, Anthony, and his wife, Angela. Anthony, as impeccably dressed as Michael, ran the investment banking division of the Stratus Meridian Group, while Michael focused on the commercial real estate division. Together, they were equal partners in the private firm. Then there was Vincent, the eldest, seated with his girlfriend, Cheryl. To Michael, Vincent carried an aura of shadow—his dealings whispered about but never openly discussed.

At the head of it all sat Dominic, their father. Once a figure in New York's mafia circles, Dominic had served five years in prison for income tax evasion—a sentence that ended more than just his freedom. It ended his ties to that life. When the family moved to Florida, Michael was fifteen, caught between adolescence and a storm of change. Dominic walked away from the old world, but its presence still clung to him, a ghost lingering in the silence around certain conversations.

The table was full—every seat claimed by family and their chosen companions. As Michael slid into his chair, he felt Bev's eyes on him. His older sister arched an eyebrow—half curiosity, half interrogation, as if preparing her next cross-examination.

"Where's your date?" she asked, suspicion lacing the question.

"Olivia was supposed to come, but she's sick," Michael answered easily.

Beverly gave him the kind of look only an older sister could—a look that said she wasn't sure whether to believe him. Michael smiled, unbothered. He hadn't lied, and that was enough. Beverly pestered him as she always did with her famous question, "When are you going to settle down?" His answer was the same as always: "Maybe never," he said with a smile, half-believing it himself.

The house lights dimmed, and the MC's voice boomed over the speakers, cutting through the chatter to announce the bridal party. Michael leaned back, watching with a detached sort of boredom as pairs of men and women he barely recognized paraded into the room arm-in-arm. It was a large party, a blur of rented tuxedos and shimmering dresses that did little to hold his attention.

That changed the moment the MC announced Charles and Verónica.

Michael straightened, his gaze snapping to the door. When she stepped into the light, it felt like the air in the room shifted. She was compact and athletic; her dress, a wash of pale green that moved against her skin like liquid silk. Every time she took a step, the high slit revealed a glimpse of toned, elegant legs balanced perfectly in her heels.

He found himself tracing the curve of her shoulders and the way her dark hair framed a face that was both delicate and strikingly strong. It was a face that demanded a second look—and a third. As if sensing his weight on her, she glanced his way. Michael let a subtle smile tug at his lips, and for a heartbeat, her deep brown eyes locked onto his.

She looked startled, almost breathless, before she jerked her gaze away, a vivid pink flush blooming across her cheeks. Michael didn't look away; he followed her all the way to the dais, unable to shake the sudden, sharp interest that hummed in his chest.

He kept watching, wondering if she was with the groomsman she had walked in with. There was no ring on her finger, but there was something about her—beyond curves and beauty—that pulled at him. Something different. Something real. She walked toward the dais, her heels clicking like soft percussion against the polished floor. Words formed in his mind as he watched her: stunning, sexy, classy. And the question lingered, unshakable: Who was she?

Throughout dinner, he caught her gaze more than once. Each time, she looked away too quickly, flushing with that soft, unmistakable shyness that intrigued him more. And each time, he smiled back, a subtle acknowledgment that he noticed, that he enjoyed being noticed.

When the music began, couples filled the dance floor. He observed the groomsman who had walked in with Verónica rise to dance with someone else. He knew then that they were not a couple. His siblings twirled with their partners, laughter rising above the band's steady rhythm. Michael's father leaned over with a half-smile.

"Not like you to just sit there, son. Find someone to dance with."

Michael grinned. He wasn't in a rush. He already knew who he wanted to dance with.

He waited, watching the bridesmaids swirl with their partners—all except her. Verónica sat alone on the dais, her expression a mix of practiced composure and quiet loneliness. After a few songs, Michael rose, straightened his jacket, and made his way across the floor with the calm confidence of a man who belonged anywhere he chose to be.

"Hi," he said when he reached her, voice warm, eyes locked on hers. "I'm Michael. I couldn't help but notice you sitting here, engaged with your phone. Would you like to dance?"

She flinched. He'd caught her off guard. He watched the heat climb as her face blushed. She looked him over, her eyes lingering on his broad shoulders as if she were seeing the kind of man women gasped about. Her mouth twitched. A small, shaky smile. She was terrified. She was hooked.

"My feet are killing me," she admitted softly.

Michael glanced down at her heels, then back up with a disarming smile. "They might be, but you look incredible in them. Come on—we'll go slow."

He watched the color rise in her cheeks, his gaze clearly unsettling her in a way she hadn't expected. It was as if he'd stirred something deep inside her that had been quiet for years. After a moment of visible hesitation, she found her resolve and gave a small nod. "Okay."

He offered his hand, steady and strong, and she let him guide her down from the dais.

On the dance floor, the band's upbeat song faded, giving way to a slow, velvety rhythm. Michael took her right hand in his left, his other hand settling carefully at the small of her back where the fabric dipped low. She tensed just for a moment. Leaning closer, he whispered, "Relax. I'll be gentle."

He spoke softly, keeping his voice steady. He saw the resistance fade from her. She leaned closer, drawn by his warmth. The wedding scene faded into the background, and the noise slipped away. He leaned in, his breath close to her ear. She trembled, and he felt it. She was his now.

"You look amazing tonight," he murmured, breath brushing her skin. "Thessaly looks beautiful in her white gown, but trust me—you're the one stealing the show. How's a gorgeous woman like you here alone?"

His words hit home. He saw her take them in. Something changed. The shy girl was gone. She met his gaze and spoke up. Her voice was steady, full of warmth. She was playing by new rules now, bold ones. He hadn't seen this fire coming, but he liked it.

"How's a man like you here alone?"

Michael chuckled softly, delighted. "I like that spunk. Truth is, I wasn't supposed to be alone. My date got sick. Guess I'm the lucky one—it brought me here, dancing with you."

He watched the way she moved, sensing a shift in her—the guardedness was gone, replaced by a raw, visible sense of being wanted. He could feel her pulse racing where his hand rested on her waist. It felt like more than just chemistry; there was a flicker of recognition in her eyes that mirrored his own. She seemed almost drunk on the moment; her edges softening under his steady gaze. He didn't look away, and he saw the exact second she stopped fighting it and simply let herself believe in the heat between them.

After a few dances, Michael leaned in, lips brushing close to her ear. "Want to get some fresh air?"

She hesitated. "Do you think it's rude to sneak outside?"

Michael's grin was quick, boyish. "Somehow, I don't think they'll miss me. You, though—you might break a few hearts. Who's going to distract all the men drooling over you?"

She laughed, cheeks flushed, whispering back, "Let's walk."

Michael offered his hand again as they stepped off the dance floor, weaving through clusters of guests laughing and clinking glasses. The night air awaited beyond the double doors—cool, fragrant with roses from the garden framing the reception hall. She took a sharp breath. The breeze hit her, and the daze in her eyes faded. She looked around as if seeing the world for the first time, as though she had just emerged from a long, dark sleep. She was finally awake. He watched as the fog lifted. She was back.

Beyond the glow of the terrace, long shadows stretched like ink across the manicured lawns, which seemed to roll endlessly into the dark. The heavy scent of damp grass and blooming jasmine hung in the cooling air, a sharp contrast to the perfume and champagne they had left behind.

The transition of sound was subtle at first, then absolute. The brassy, rhythmic pulse of the live band began to dissolve into a hazy echo, losing its battle against the night's natural symphony. In its place, the steady, rhythmic chirping of crickets rose from the tall grass—a primal, ancient chant that filled the silence. Each step they took further muffled the party's festive noise until the only sounds left were their shoes beneath their feet and the steady beat of their own breathing.

A sudden, sharp breeze picked up, causing the fine hairs on Verónica's arms to stand on end. Before she could shiver, he was there. He moved with quiet grace, lifting his jacket and draping it carefully over her shoulders. He heard the catch in her throat as the heavy fabric, still holding the heat of his body, settled over her. She huddled into the cedar-scented wool as if seeking a hiding place, her world narrowing down to the two of them. As her fingers brushed the silk lining of his lapels, she looked up, finally noticing just how close he was standing—close enough that there was nowhere else for her to look.

"Better?" he asked, his voice lower now, intimate against the stillness.

She nodded, avoiding his eyes at first. "Yes, thank you."

Michael stepped closer, not crowding her, but enough that she felt the pull of his presence—the warmth radiating from him, the gravity of his confidence, the scent of his cologne. "I have to say," he murmured, "I wasn't expecting tonight to be memorable. I figured I'd show my face, make my dad happy, and leave early. But then I saw you."

A sudden stillness came over her. Michael could see her struggling to believe him, even as a desperate hope took hold. The lights glinted in her eyes as she turned her head. "You don't even know me," she whispered, the words hanging in the air like something fragile that might break if he moved too quickly.

Michael's gaze held hers, steady and unwavering. "That's the thing. I want to."

Chapter 3

Verónica

For a moment, silence hung between them—charged, delicate, trembling with possibilities. Verónica could hear the faint hum of cicadas in the distance, the muffled laughter spilling from inside. But here, outside, it felt as though the world had narrowed to just the two of them.

"You're dangerous," she said finally, though there was a smile tugging at her lips.

"Why's that?"

"Because men like you don't notice women like me."

Michael tilted his head, studying her with a sharpness that made her pulse quicken. "That's where you're wrong. I noticed you the second you walked in—and I haven't looked away since."

Her breath caught. The vulnerability inside her, the years of feeling less-than, flickered against the sheer weight of his attention. She wanted to deflect, to laugh it off, but instead, she held his gaze, letting herself believe him—just this once.

Somewhere deep down, Verónica knew this moment would change her. Maybe it was temporary, maybe it was fleeting, but standing under the glow of string lights with Michael's eyes fixed on her, she felt something she hadn't in years—seen, wanted, alive.

Verónica had spent eight years tethered to a man who never truly saw her. Not in the way that mattered. Desire, intimacy, fulfillment—those were foreign lands she'd only read about, never visited. Sex had been a one-sided ritual: his release, his silence, his back turned before she could even exhale. Her own needs were ghosts in the room, unacknowledged and uninvited.

Now, standing before Michael, she felt a flicker of something unfamiliar—possibility, maybe even hope. But doubt crept in just as quickly. Would he be any different? Or was this just another prelude to disappointment? For the first time, the question echoed louder than her longing: Were all men the same?

And that thought unsettled her more than she expected.

Michael leaned against the railing, casual yet commanding, his tailored shirt exposing his athletic physique. He looked at her, really looked, with a focus that made her chest tighten.

"You know," he said with a small smile, "I rarely enjoy weddings. But tonight feels... different."

Verónica lowered her eyes, feeling heat rise in her cheeks. "Different how?"

"Because of you."

The words hung between them, impossibly simple yet heavy enough to tilt her world. He reached out and brushed his fingers against her hand, where it rested on the railing. The contact was fleeting, almost cautious—but it sent a jolt through her. Before she could think, she let her hand stay there, her palm trembling slightly beneath his warmth.

Her mind spun, questioning her own impulses. She had never been reckless, never the type to fall into a man's arms on a whim. For years, Gregory's voice had lived inside her—cutting, cold, telling her she wasn't enough. And yet here was Michael, the kind of man other women whispered about, standing inches from her, looking at her as if she were the only person alive.

He intertwined his fingers with hers, firm but gentle, and her breath caught. Every part of her wanted to pull away, to retreat into the safety of what she knew. But another part—a part long buried—was begging to lean in, to taste the danger of desire.

Michael's voice dropped low, velvet against the night air. "You feel this too, don't you?"

She swallowed hard, her heart racing. She did, and with that realization came a thought that both thrilled and terrified her: Could she allow herself to let go just once, to experience something wild and unforgettable—even if only for a single night?

The question lingered, unspoken but alive, as she met his gaze.

Michael's hand was still clasped around hers, steady, certain, while her own pulse hammered in her wrist. He didn't pull, didn't rush, just held her—as if giving her the choice. His restraint only made the tension coil tighter inside her.

"I can feel your heart racing," he whispered, leaning just close enough that his scent brushed her nose. "Tell me if I'm wrong."

She laughed softly, nervous, a little breathless. "You're not wrong."

Her body betrayed her with every signal: the warmth spreading through her chest, the way her lips parted, the sudden ache low in her stomach. She hadn't felt this alive in years. And yet, a voice in her head screamed for caution. Don't do this. Don't be that woman. Don't ruin the fragile balance you've rebuilt.

But another voice, louder now, rose from somewhere deeper: Why not? Why not feel wanted, even just once? Why not let go of the years of being invisible?

Michael leaned in and asked, "Would you like to find someplace to sit and talk?"

She met his gaze, a small smile curving her lips. "That sounds nice," she said, surprised by how easily the words came.

Michael, still holding her hand, his touch confident yet unassuming, turned, and together they wandered along the terrace. Warm air drifted around them as their footsteps slowed, the noise of the evening fading behind them until they reached a cluster of tables tucked just outside the terrace restaurant's entrance. Only one was occupied—a trio leaning close in quiet conversation, their laughter subdued.

Without a word, Michael guided her to a table set far enough away to offer privacy. He pulled out her chair before taking his own, his attention focused entirely on her, as though the rest of the night had narrowed to this single space between them.

Verónica wasn't accustomed to that kind of care. Men rarely paused to consider her thoughts, her feelings, or what she might want to say next. Yet something about Michael made her feel noticed—valued in a way that went beyond appearance. Sitting across from him, she felt unexpectedly at ease, as if opening up were not a risk but a natural response.

She began talking about her ex-husband, Gregory. How she'd married him so young while still in college, believing it would last forever. How she'd always dreamed of having children and raising a family. Her sister used to reassure her, "He'll come around. Give him time." It was easy for her to say—she had three kids. "Of course I adore them," Verónica added softly.

Gregory would always say, "We're not ready for kids." What he really meant was he wasn't ready—too busy running around with his secretary. Verónica's voice tightened as she muttered sarcastically, "I hope he's happy with her now."

Michael didn't interrupt. He just listened, eyes locked on hers—something Verónica wasn't accustomed to. Something Gregory would never do. Finally, he smiled and said, "From what I'm hearing, the only conclusion I can draw is that Gregory's a complete moron." Then, with a playful grin, he added, "I have no clue what his secretary looks like, but I can tell you from where I sit—she's got nothing on you."

Verónica's eyes widened, her heart racing. Could this gorgeous, sexy god of a man really see her that way, or was he merely saying things to make someone like her feel better?

Michael leaned back and said, "Let's get a nice bottle of champagne and enjoy this beautiful evening as we talk." She smiled. "I'm not a big drinker, and I've already had two, but what the hell—tonight's a celebration."

The terrace belonged to the hotel hosting the reception. Michael nodded to a server, who approached promptly. "Yes, sir. What can I get you?" Michael replied. "How about a vintage bottle of Veuve Clicquot La Grande Dame Rosé?" "Yes, sir. Let me check."

Verónica, who lived paycheck to paycheck and rarely drank, had no idea what Michael had just ordered—but it sounded expensive. The server returned with an ice bucket and set everything up. Verónica took a sip, marveling at the champagne—spectacular, unlike anything she had tasted before. She was always happy with a fifteen-dollar bottle of champagne.

Verónica leaned in slightly, her voice gentle but curious. "Was the woman who got sick tonight... your girlfriend?"

Michael laughed softly, the sound low and warm. "No, not at all. If I had a girlfriend, I wouldn't be sitting here, enjoying your company as much as I am."

The words settled between them like a quiet breeze, brushing against something tender in her chest. She smiled, a little caught off guard by the sincerity in his tone. "Still... how does a man like you not have a girlfriend?"

He gave a slow, thoughtful smile. "Maybe because I lose track of time chasing deadlines and projects. My sister keeps telling me I need to slow down, find someone who makes me want to stay still for a while. But I guess the right person hasn't come along yet. Or maybe..." He paused, eyes meeting hers with a flicker of something unspoken. "Maybe I just enjoy being in the moment and not looking for tomorrow."

Verónica felt her breath catch. There was something in the way he said it—not rehearsed, not careless. Just honest.

Michael leaned forward slightly, his voice low and thoughtful. "Haven't you ever just... let yourself enjoy the moment with someone? Without worrying about tomorrow?"

Verónica paused, her gaze drifting to the flicker of candlelight between them. She searched the question, then answered quietly, "No."

Michael blinked, surprised. "Wow."

She hesitated, then added, almost in a whisper, "I've never been with another man besides Gregory. I'm sure that sounds ridiculous to someone like you."

His expression softened, the teasing charm replaced by something gentler. "No," he said, shaking his head slowly. "It doesn't sound ridiculous. It sounds... precious."

Verónica's breath caught at the word. Precious. It wrapped around her like a warm blanket she hadn't realized she needed. Gregory had spent years convincing her she wasn't enough—too quiet, too needy, too forgettable.

And yet here was Michael, looking at her as if she were something rare. Something very special.

"Have you ever been married?" Verónica asked, her voice casual but her eyes searching.

Michael shook his head. "No. Never felt the urge."

"Have you ever come close?" she pressed.

Michael seemed to consider the question for a moment. "I guess I have—once. But I quickly realized it wasn't going to work."

"Can I ask why not?" she said softly.

Michael's lips curved into a smile. "Did my sister put you up to this?"

Verónica blinked, caught off guard. "No, of course not."

He chuckled, the sound warm and teasing. "It just sounds like the questions my sister always asks me. She never misses a chance." Then, more seriously, he added, "I guess the truth is, I've been focused on work—on building something that will last. I haven't had much time for relationships."

Verónica studied him in silence for a moment. He was gorgeous, sexy, and sweet—everything one could want. And yet here he was, talking to her. She tried to steady herself, reminding her heart of what her mind already knew: this had to remain a one-night encounter.

Michael tilted his head, his gaze holding hers. "Do you focus on work? What do you do?"

"I'm an attorney," she replied. "I just started a new job six months ago. I'd given up my career before that—to support Gregory in his business. I was his gofer, really. I stayed home, did all the support work, while he spent his time in the office with his secretary." Her voice tightened. "I had no idea how much of a fool I was being."

Michael shook his head firmly. "That's one way to see it. But not how I see it."

Verónica narrowed her eyes, intrigued despite herself. "Then how do you see it?"

"As I said before," Michael replied, his tone steady, almost protective. "Gregory must be a complete moron. He lost you—and he's too dumb to realize what he gave up. One thing I learned a long time ago: when you find something of value, you hold on to it. Because value," he leaned in slightly, his eyes never leaving hers, "always increases."

Verónica's heart skipped as she struggled to believe his words. Could a man who looked like he stepped out of a sculptor's dream really mean this? Was she being a fool, or was he sincere?

They talked until 1:00 a.m., losing track of time. Minutes turned into hours, and before they realized it, the music from the wedding had faded into silence. They stood and walked a few steps back toward the reception doors, stopping at the railing again.

Michael reached up and brushed a stray lock of hair from her face, his fingertips grazing her skin with deliberate care. She closed her eyes at the touch, then opened them to find him watching her with that dangerous, devastating focus—the look that stripped away all pretense.

"If I kiss you right now," he murmured, "would you stop me?"

Verónica's breath hitched. Her mind screamed a dozen reasons to step back, to laugh it off, to retreat into safety. But her body, her heart, every fragile piece of her that had been starving for this kind of attention, whispered just one word: No.

She shook her head—barely, but enough.

Michael didn't move right away. He gave her a chance to change her mind, to pull away. Instead, she leaned closer, her hand tightening in his as though her body had already decided for her.

The kiss, when it came, was slow, unhurried, but it ignited something raw and consuming. Verónica clung to him, stunned by her own boldness. Inside, her thoughts raced: Am I really doing this? Am I really about to step into something I've never dared before?

The answer pulsed in every shiver that ran through her body. She hadn't felt this alive, this desired, in years. For the first time, the thought surfaced that one night of surrender might not be a mistake—but a salvation.

The kiss lingered, deepened, and when it finally broke, Verónica felt her entire body trembling. She had never been kissed like that before. She searched his eyes, half-expecting to see amusement or pity, but instead there was only raw want—and something steadier, something that told her he wasn't playing a game.

Her lips parted, but words failed her. She wanted to ask what they were doing, where this was leading, but she already knew. The answer pulsed between them like electricity.

Michael brushed his thumb across her hand, still holding it as though anchoring her to the moment. "We don't have to," he said quietly, his voice low, controlled. "But if you want to get out of here…" He left it hanging, no pressure, no rush—just an invitation.

Her chest tightened. Every rational thought screamed for her to smile politely, thank him, and go back inside. She was a divorcee still bleeding from betrayal, a woman who had built walls so high she had nearly forgotten how to feel. But here she was, standing in the cool night air with a man who made those walls crumble with nothing more than a look.

"I shouldn't," she whispered.

Michael leaned closer, close enough that his lips brushed her ear. "Sometimes the things we shouldn't do are the ones we need most."

The words stole her breath. Her fingers tightened around his instinctively, and she realized she wasn't letting go.

She remembered Susan saying to her, "You only live once, Verónica. What if you never get another chance?"

"Your place or mine?" she heard herself ask, the boldness shocking her even as she said it.

Michael's slow, captivating smile sealed it. He didn't answer right away—just pulled her closer, pressing a soft kiss against her lips. Then, with his arm slipping firmly around her waist, Michael guided her toward the row of gleaming cars waiting at the hotel's curb. Headlights shimmered like jewels against the night, but one in particular made Verónica's breath hitch—a brand-new, fire-red Ferrari, top down, saddle leather interior, that seemed to glow under the streetlamps.

As they approached, the valet was moving before they even reached the curb, grabbing a key and swinging open the passenger door. Verónica froze, staring at the sleek machine in disbelief. She had only ever seen cars like this streaking down the highway or gracing the glossy pages of a magazine. Now, impossibly, she was about to slide into one—Michael's Ferrari.

Each step away from the reception hall felt like stepping out of her old life—out of the shadows of Gregory's betrayal, out of the years of invisibility—and into something frightening, reckless, and thrillingly alive.

She knew it was madness. She knew she might regret it come morning. And yet, as she slid into the soft leather seat beside him, she also knew one truth with absolute clarity: for tonight, she wanted to be his, and his alone.

Chapter 4

Verónica

They drove a short distance to his building in downtown Miami. When the car pulled up, the doorman rushed forward with polished efficiency. Michael slipped out and moved to open Verónica's door, but the doorman beat him to it.

"Good evening, Mr. Marino," the man greeted warmly.

"Good evening, George," Michael replied with his serene confidence, handing him the key to the car.

The building towered above them, all marble and glass glowing with soft golden light. Inside, the lobby shimmered with polished stone and muted chandeliers, every surface gleaming like wealth itself. Michael's hand slid into Verónica's as though it belonged there, his touch steady, claiming, and she followed, her heels clicking against the marble, each sound echoing the erratic pounding of her heart.

In the elevator, silence fell heavy, thick with anticipation. Michael tapped his key card against the sleek black pad, and the doors slid shut with a soft hiss. The space felt intimate—too small for the electricity between them. Verónica felt the heat radiating from his body, close enough that a single breath might bridge the distance. Her pulse leapt when he finally turned, his gaze locking onto hers, steady and unreadable. Slowly, deliberately, he reached out, brushing a strand of hair from her cheek. Then, with a reverence that made her skin hum, he placed a kiss on her lips—feather-light, almost hesitant, but it ignited something deep and undeniable.

The elevator chimed, and the doors opened—not to a hallway, but directly into his penthouse. The rest of the world seemed to fall away.

Her breath caught—part nerves, part hunger—as she stepped into the space.

Floor-to-ceiling windows wrapped around the living room like a glass cocoon, revealing Miami glittering below in a mosaic of light. The city looked unreal from this height—like a dream stitched together with neon and moonlight. The air smelled faintly of salt and expensive cologne. Everything was curated: marble floors, low-slung Italian furniture, a wall of abstract art lit like a gallery. It was breathtaking—unreal—but what made her heart race wasn't the view. It was him.

For a moment, questions surged. What did this man do to live like this? Was he a gangster? A drug dealer? Something darker? But then he looked at her—really looked—and the doubts dissolved under the heat in his eyes. Whatever he was, she was already too far in to turn back.

Michael shrugged off his jacket and draped it neatly over a chair. When he turned back, he stepped in close, his arms slipping around her waist, pulling her softly but firmly against him. His voice was low, controlled, but his eyes betrayed the fire beneath.

"If you want me to stop," he said, each word deliberate, "tell me now."

For a moment, Verónica couldn't breathe. She had never done anything like this, not once. Gregory's voice—cold, dismissive, belittling—whispered in the back of her mind, telling her she wasn't good enough, that no one would ever want her. But Michael's gaze drowned it all out. He was looking at her as if she were the only woman in existence, as if she were enough.

Her hand trembled as she placed it against his chest, feeling the solid strength of him beneath the fine fabric. Her voice was barely a whisper, but it carried every ounce of courage she had.

"Don't stop."

The restraint in his eyes broke into a smile, a slow, hungry curve that sent heat spiraling through her. His arms closed around her fully; his lips met hers. The kiss was tentative at first, savoring, then deepened, urgent and consuming. The taste of him, the warmth of his mouth, his tongue, the press of his body—it was overwhelming, a rush of sensations that unraveled her.

The apartment seemed to dissolve. The muted hum of the city outside, the soft glow of the lamp, the polished perfection of the room—all of it blurred until there was only him. His hands traced the lines of her back, pulling her closer until there was no space left between them.

When he swept her up into his arms, she gasped, then clung to him, her heart pounding against his chest. He carried her down the hallway with sure, unhurried steps, as if he had all the time in the world to claim her. In the bedroom, a king-sized bed waited—sheets crisp, white, untouched. A single lamp cast amber light over the space, throwing shadows that flickered across the walls like fire. Soft music played in the background.

Tonight was no longer about hesitation. Tonight was about surrender.

Verónica's breath came unevenly; her pulse was wild. She could hardly believe this was happening; she was happening. For so long, she had lived locked inside herself, convinced she was undeserving of desire. Yet now, standing in Michael's arms, with his gaze taking her in as though she were the only woman alive, she felt more than wanted. She felt powerful.

His fingers brushed along her jaw, then down the side of her neck, sending shivers cascading through her body. When his lips met hers again, the kiss was no longer tentative—it was hungry, urgent, claiming. She melted against him, her hands clutching his shirt, pulling him closer until there was no space left between them. The world outside dissolved; only the heat of him remained.

He guided her toward the bed, every step punctuated by another kiss, another stolen breath. When she stumbled slightly, laughing against his mouth, he steadied her, whispering, "I've got you." The words were low, steady, a promise that rippled through her like fire.

At the bedside, Michael's hands framed Verónica's face, searching her eyes one last time. "Verónica..." he murmured, as though her name itself were an invocation. She answered not with words but by slipping her hand into his, pressing it to her heart. The message was clear: I'm yours. Tonight, I'm yours.

When he drew her down onto the cool, white sheets, nerves still rippled through her body, faint shadows of doubt clinging to her like cobwebs. What does he see in me? What if he expects someone else—someone experienced, someone flawless? The thought gnawed at her, tormenting her with Gregory's old words, the ones that had branded her as inadequate, unworthy. For a fleeting moment, she almost believed them again.

But then Michael's lips grazed her collarbone, slow and reverent, his hands exploring her with patience instead of urgency. He wasn't demanding perfection; he was savoring her. Every kiss, every gentle stroke of his fingertips, unraveled the years of neglect that had hollowed her confidence. His whispered words—soft, steady, certain—sank deeper than desire.

She closed her eyes and let herself follow his lead, surrendering inch by inch. The world outside fell away. There was no Gregory, no loneliness, no haunting questions of why wasn't I enough? There was only this: the warmth of Michael's body pressed to hers, the rhythm of his breath against her skin, the undeniable truth that in this moment—here, now—she was not just enough. She was wanted. Desired. Alive!

Verónica lay quietly on her back, enveloped in a profound sense of bliss. Michael's lips pressed against hers with a passion that sent waves of exhilaration through her. As he traced kisses down her neck, each touch ignited a deeper fire within her. She felt his hands gently unclasp her dress; the fabric slipping down her body, revealing her bare skin. She caught the way his smile grew as he saw her exposed breast, unshielded by a bra. The vulnerability of being so exposed under his steady focus sent a wave of tenderness through her.

His kisses moved deliberately, tender yet fervent, from one breast to the other, eliciting a flush of heat and desire. Verónica's breath caught, her moans growing more insistent, betraying the building intensity she felt. As Michael peeled the dress completely away, his whispered compliments on her beauty wrapped around her like a warm embrace. He slowly removed her heels, one first, then the other, kissing each foot reverently, as if honoring a sacred part of her.

His mouth journeyed upward again, and Verónica's moans turned into urgent pleas. When his hand found the silk thong she wore to smooth her silhouette, soaked with her arousal, a shiver ran through her. His fingers slipped beneath the delicate fabric, exploring her intimately, and the sound she released was raw and uninhibited. Her body responded instinctively, every touch sending waves of pleasure coursing through her.

Michael slowly removed her thong, and his lips began tasting her with reverence, his fingers moving inside her, evoking shivers of ecstasy. His thumb caressed her sweet spot with a rhythm that seemed perfectly attuned to her needs. "Please don't stop," she begged, her voice trembling with need.

His reply was steady and sincere, devoid of hesitation. "I have no intention of stopping until you are completely satisfied." The words struck her deeply, stirring emotions she had never dared to hope for—a promise of devotion and care.

The intensity built rapidly as Michael's fingers and mouth worked in harmony. Verónica's cries grew louder, her body tensing as she reached a climax unlike any she had known—deep, consuming, and lasting, leaving her physically spent yet emotionally soaring. Michael rose, trailing kisses along her body, and as their eyes met, she whispered, "I can't believe how you made me feel." His smile was confident, full of promise. "The night is young; we have just begun."

Their lips met again in a passionate kiss. When they parted, Michael chuckled softly, "See how magnificent you taste." Verónica's cheeks flushed with a mix of shyness and desire. "I want more of you," she admitted, the words tasting like liberation.

Despite the intimacy, Michael remained clothed except for his shirt. He stood, and Verónica's gaze traced the lines of his chest and abs, her breath catching at the sight. As he shed his pants and underwear, revealing his arousal, she whispered again, awestruck, "Oh my God." He returned to the bed, pressing against her, and she couldn't resist the urge to touch him, confessing, "It's so hard, I want to feel you inside me now." The honesty surprised even her, but Michael's presence had unlocked a new realm of feeling within her.

She watched him reach for the nightstand; the deliberate way he retrieved the condom only heightened her anticipation. As he rolled it on, his gaze dipped down, and the knowing smile that touched his lips told her he could see exactly how much she wanted him. He drew her closer, and she lifted her knees instinctively, inviting him in. The initial entry was slow, a tender exploration that made her moan with a sharp, sweet pleasure. As he moved deeper, her grip on him tightened, pulling him closer still, her voice breaking into urgent cries. "Don't stop, Michael... please don't stop."

Michael whispered, "I'm not stopping—I want to savor every moment with you." Gently, he took her hands and raised them above her head, stretching them to their fullest across the bed with his body lying on top of her. His movements were slow, deliberate; each thrust deep and purposeful. Her moans grew more urgent, filling the room with raw desire. "Oh my God, you feel incredible," she breathed. Pressing his body against hers, his lips brushed over her nipples, hardened like polished stones. "You have a magnificent body," he murmured, his voice thick with admiration. Sensations she had never experienced before overwhelmed Verónica. Gradually, he lifted himself slightly and captured her nipples with his mouth, sucking them tenderly while continuing his deep, rhythmic thrusts. Her moans escalated into urgent pleas. "Harder, harder." Responding, his thrusts grew more forceful, hands lifting her butt in sync with the rhythm, driving her toward another ecstatic climax. Her screams echoed her awe and gratitude; her body trembling with the intensity of the moment. Michael's own release was powerful; he lay on her for a moment, then withdrew, settling beside her, their bodies tangled, his lips brushing hers with gentle affection. "That was amazing. You are truly an amazing woman," he murmured. She smiled and said, "My legs are still shaking."

In the quiet that followed, Verónica rested her cheek against his chest, listening to the steady beat of his heart, feeling the comforting warmth of his arms. The city outside stretched vast and indifferent, but inside this room, the world had shrunk to a perfect, intimate sphere. For this night—this precious, transformative night—Verónica allowed herself to believe she was not just enough, but more than enough.

An hour later, the spark between them flared back into a consuming fire, neither willing to surrender to fatigue. They moved together with a hunger that felt both urgent and unending, each touch drawing Verónica higher until she was adrift in a place she'd never known existed.

Outside, the world lay silent and dark; the hour was creeping toward 4:00 a.m., but inside, time seemed suspended. Only when their bodies finally stilled, hearts slowing in unison, did they drift into sleep—tangled in each other's warmth, the faint promise of dawn still hours away.

Chapter 5

Michael

At the stroke of 7:30 a.m., Michael's eyes fluttered open, betraying the scant three and a half hours of sleep he had stolen. He turned, stealing a glance at Verónica, who lay beside him in serene slumber, her beauty untouched by the early sun. She looked so innocent and beautiful that it struck him. Guests overnight were a rarity for him—he preferred the fleeting pleasures before sleep time, whisking them away with a driver waiting in the wings. Yet, with Verónica, an unspoken hesitation held him captive; the usual urge to send her away was absent, replaced by a magnetic pull he couldn't explain.

Silently, he slipped from the bed, careful not to disturb her delicate rest, and made his way to the bathroom. Returning, his gaze met hers—awake, watching him with a tender smile that stirred something deep within him.

"I thought you were sleeping," he murmured, his voice thick with quiet surprise.

Her eyes twinkled mischievously. "I woke up when I realized your body wasn't next to mine."

Without hesitation, he settled back beside her, pressing his lips to hers in a kiss that spoke of longing and unspoken promises. She pulled away briefly, cheeks flushed, whispering, "I must have morning breath."

He chuckled softly, tilting her face back to capture her lips again. "To me, you taste like the sweetest temptation. But if it eases your mind, there's an extra toothbrush in the bathroom—I did brush mine, after all."

She sat up in bed, holding the sheet over her breasts, hesitating. "I don't have anything to wear."

Michael's gaze roamed over her flawless face, a slow smile curving his lips. "Isn't that the most delightful predicament? I get to savor every move of your gorgeous body in the daylight."

A playful frown crossed her face, but he merely shrugged and disappeared briefly, returning with a soft T-shirt. Handing it to her, he said, "Here."

"Thank you," she breathed. "I enjoyed the view of your little walk-about."

When she returned, standing by the bed, she announced her intention to leave. Michael countered smoothly, "Let's have breakfast first. I'll call it in." But before that, he held out his hand. She took it, and he pulled her gently down on the bed, saying, "I need an encore of last night."

Their lips met again, deep and urgent, tongues weaving a fiery dance as the T-shirt slipped to the floor. His hands explored the curves of her body all over again, eliciting soft moans that sent heat rippling between them. He let his mouth drift lower, his lips skimming the velvet skin of her chest until he reached the swell of her breasts. There, her nipples stood proud and hard, reacting to the heat of his breath. The Miami sun poured through the glass in a brilliant flood of gold, catching the fine sheen of perspiration on her skin and making her glisten like polished marble. To Michael, she looked as if she were being forged in the light itself—vibrant, luminous, and entirely his for the taking. He lingered there for a heartbeat, mesmerized by the way the morning radiance turned her body into a masterpiece of curves and shadows before he leaned in to taste her.

Michael let his hand wander lower, charting the silk-smooth skin of her inner thighs until he found the center of her womanhood. She was already slick, her body yielding to him with an eagerness that sent a surge of dark satisfaction through his chest. With the steady, practiced rhythm of a man who knew exactly how to dismantle a woman's defenses, he began to work. His thumb found the delicate bundle of nerves at her peak, circling with a calculated pressure that drew a sharp, hitching breath from her lungs. He watched her through the shadows, mesmerized by the way her head fell back and her arched throat bared itself to him.

As he coaxed her higher, her poise from earlier in the evening shattered completely. She was now a woman trembling on the edge of a precipice. "Please don't stop… don't stop. I have never felt anything like this," she begged, her voice a ragged whisper that vibrated against his skin. Michael knew she was in ecstasy again as he felt the desperate pull of her hands in his hair, her fingers clenching as his tongue went deep inside her, while his thumb maintained its relentless, spiraling pace on her sweet spot. He could feel the internal rhythm of her body quickening, the muscles of her thighs tensing as she climbed toward a peak that seemed to catch her by surprise, as if she had never expected to find this kind of intensity in his arms.

She looked completely lost in the sensation; her moans growing into beautiful, desperate cries that filled the quiet room. When her climax finally hit, it was violent and total. He felt the rhythmic waves of her release squeezing his finger as she shattered, her breath leaving her in a long, shuddering sob of pure ecstasy. As she collapsed back against the pillows, utterly spent and eyes glazed with wonder, Michael looked up, watching the way she looked at him. There was a newfound hunger in her expression, a look that suggested the life she'd lived before this moment had suddenly lost its color. He knew, with a quiet sense of triumph, that he had shown her something she didn't know existed.

Michael leaned in, their eyes locking—hers glowing with newfound passion and contentment. She drew him close, lips crashing against his in a fierce, hungry kiss. "I need you once more," she whispered, "but first, I want to taste you."

She straddled him, hands roaming, lips tracing a fiery path from neck to hardened flesh. She licked his length on each side, eliciting more moans from him. Then she placed her lips on his tip and slowly took him in. Her touch was reverent yet eager, coaxing a powerful pulse from him. Just as he neared the edge, she stopped and whispered, "I need you inside me."

With a practiced hand, Michael donned a condom, then positioned her on all fours, entering her from behind. Her moans crescendoed, filling the room with raw, unfiltered desire as he moved with increasing intensity. The more he filled her, the more she moaned. Until, bringing her closer to climax, she said, "Deeper, deeper." He pulled her in as close as he could from her hips, and she exploded with more loud yells, causing him to pump harder until he exploded with a powerful thrust, his body shuddering against hers.

"You are incredible," he murmured into her ear, holding her close as they collapsed into a tangled heap.

They lay there, bodies slick with sweat and ecstasy, hearts pounding in unison, breathing in the quiet aftermath of their passion. Eventually, Michael broke the silence. Smiling, he said, "Let me order breakfast. We need the energy."

Breakfast arrived within the hour. Between bites and laughter, they showered away the night's heat and the morning's passion. Verónica confessed she had nothing to wear home but her bridesmaid dress. Michael smiled. "You look stunning in it, but let me find you something more comfortable."

He returned with oversized sweats and another T-shirt, which she donned with a playful shrug, the fabric draping loosely over her curves.

As the morning waned and they finished breakfast, she prepared to leave. "Thank you," she said softly, "for a night I'll never forget. You awakened something in me I never thought possible."

Michael smiled knowingly. "Gregory is an idiot."

He summoned his car and driver, and as she embraced him goodbye, a strange hesitation kept him from asking for her number. Why? Perhaps fear—fear of someone as extraordinary as her.

He sank onto the couch, the memory of their night still burning within him, grateful yet restless, craving the impossible again.

Chapter 6

Verónica

When the elevator doors slid open, a large, well-dressed man stood waiting as though he had been snatched from a Hollywood movie script. His black suit hugged his broad shoulders, and his expression was perfectly neutral, professional. "Ms. Verónica," he said with a polite nod.

She blinked, startled, but managed a small smile.

"My name is Grant. Please follow me. I am your ride home."

The words carried a quiet authority, and without hesitation, she followed him through the glittering lobby and out into the Miami sun. A sleek black Range Rover idled at the curb, polished to a mirror shine. When he opened the door, the subtle scent of new leather greeted her, warm and expensive.

She sank into the plush back seat, the leather cool against her skin, and tried to relax, though her body hummed with restless energy. Her mind reeled, looping through the night on repeat. What had just happened? She had been ushered into a new world, one she never imagined existed outside of movies or whispered fantasies. Her legs were still weak, as if they remembered his touch long after it had ended. And Michael—his cologne, his heat, his lips—still clung to her like a secret she couldn't wash away.

When Grant pulled up to her building, he slipped from the driver's seat and opened her door with flawless composure. He waited as she stepped out, his gaze steady but unreadable.

"Is everything okay?" she asked, suddenly aware of how vulnerable she must have looked in that moment—rumpled, dazed, utterly undone in Michael's sweatpants and T-shirt, carrying her gown.

"Fine, ma'am," he said evenly. "I was told to make sure you arrived home safe. I'll wait until you're inside."

Something in his tone—professional yet protective—sent a flicker of warmth through her. Michael had thought of this. Michael had arranged this. She smiled faintly, murmured her thanks, and disappeared into her building, all the while wondering: Is he always this considerate? Or was it just for her?

Later, sprawled across her bed, she stared at the ceiling as waves of memory washed over her. Michael had made her feel things she hadn't even known she was capable of feeling. Every kiss, every touch, every careful moment of pleasure—he had taken his time, as though she were not just another conquest, but a woman worth savoring. She had never felt so desired, so seen.

Part of her wanted to tell the entire world, to shout it into the night. And another part of her wanted to bury it deep, keep it locked away as hers alone, too fragile to share. She wished, with an ache that hollowed her out, that her mother was still alive. Her mother would have understood. She knew what it was to be cherished, to love and be loved in return. She had it with her father, what Verónica thought she would have with Gregory.

But with Gregory, it could never have been. He had always seemed too selfish, too blind to anything beyond his own reflection. He had never once shown her that he cared what she needed, and he certainly never asked if she was satisfied or happy. Michael was everything Gregory was not. Everything she thought a man could never be—until last night.

She pressed her fingers to her lips, remembering. She wouldn't trade those hours with Michael for anything. To have gone through life without ever experiencing that raw, consuming passion—the kind that makes you feel as if you've finally learned to breathe—would have been a tragedy.

And yet, as the adrenaline faded, sadness settled in. It was a one-night stand. Michael hadn't even asked for her number. If he had wanted to see her again, surely he would have. Of course, he could easily track her down through Thessaly—but he wouldn't. Because this was what he told her he lived for: the moment. Not tomorrow. No promises. Not relationships. Just now.

Still, knowing that didn't make the emptiness easier to swallow. Because deep down, she wanted him again. And again.

She moved to lean her head on the pillow, closing her eyes to catch the fading scent of him, but a sharp, metallic click punctured the moment. It was just the central AC kicking on, but the sound drew her gaze toward the corner of the room where her heavy leather briefcase sat slumped on a chair, its gold buckles glinting like cold, mocking eyes. Beside it, her laptop bag was stuffed to bursting with prospective files for possible new clients—a physical manifestation of the life she was neglecting.

Verónica exhaled sharply, the sound cutting through the quiet of her apartment as she forced herself upright. She felt the warmth and softness leave her face, replaced by the familiar, tight pull of professional anxiety. She couldn't afford to spiral into these memories; she needed to find her focus, or at least the shadow of it. The pressure was a physical weight, pressing into her temples with a dull, insistent throb.

How was she supposed to conjure new business out of thin air? The absurdity of their demands tasted like ash in her mouth. She wondered if they expected her to hike up her skirt and stand on a Miami street corner like some kind of high-priced solicitor, begging passersby to let her litigate their lives. It was a humiliating thought, yet as she stared at the mountain of work waiting for her, the line between the prestigious halls of her firm and the desperation of the street felt thinner than ever.

Susan would have known exactly what to do. She would be at every cocktail party, every networking mixer, charming clients with her laughter and her dangerous allure. Verónica knew her friend's way—if Susan wanted an account badly enough, she'd fuck her way into it—or more if she needed to. That was just the way Susan lived.

But that wasn't hers. What she did last night with Michael—she did that for herself. To fill the hollow space inside, to remember that she was still alive. Not for money, not for leverage. Never that.

No, she wasn't Thessaly. She wasn't Susan. She was just Verónica.

Last night had changed the narrative, offering a glimpse of something she didn't dare believe before. Michael's attention proved she was desirable, that she possessed a pull she hadn't recognized in herself. It left her with the lingering thought that maybe, one day, she would find a man who looked at her that way and decided he never wanted to let go.

She rolled onto her side, burying her face in the pillow. But the scent of him was still there—faint, intoxicating, impossible to escape. It was like he had branded her, not with words, not with promises, but with the memory of his touch.

She told herself she had to move on, that this was nothing more than a fleeting moment in a life that demanded discipline and order. But as her eyelids grew heavy, one truth whispered back at her, stubborn and unrelenting.

She didn't just want to be desired. She wanted him.

And no matter how much she tried to silence it, the thought of Michael lingered—dangerous, sweet, and undeniable—like the echo of a song she knew she'd never forget.

Chapter 7

Michael

Michael woke from the nap he had taken on the couch after Verónica left. For a long moment, he just lay there, staring at the ceiling, his body still humming with the memory of her. What had happened the night before was unlike anything he had experienced in years. It had been raw, intense, and consuming. He replayed every moment—the way her lips had trembled under his, the sound of her moans filling the room, the warmth of her body arching against his. He could still taste her pleasure, still smell the sweetness of her skin.

But then came the question—the one that pressed hard against his chest. Why was he so absorbed with her? What was it about her that made it different? Being intimate with a woman wasn't unfamiliar territory. He had been with more women than he cared to count. Usually, he walked away without a second thought, no guilt, no lingering what-ifs. Yet with her, something clung to him, something that refused to be brushed aside.

He told himself to forget her. He didn't have the time, and he knew Verónica wasn't a casual type of woman. She deserved someone who could give her more than stolen hours and whispered promises. That wasn't him. At least, that's what he kept telling himself. Still, part of him was glad—glad he had given her a night of passion she clearly hadn't known before. Glad he had shown her what it felt like to be wanted, to be adored. He ran a hand through his hair and sat up, shaking his head. "Snap out of it," he muttered. "Time to get ready for Sunday dinner at Dad's."

Michael stepped into his father's house, the heavy scent of roasted garlic and seasoned meat acting as a more effective greeting than the chorus of voices drifting from the dining room. As he rounded the corner, the familiar tableau of the family table opened up before him. They were all there. His niece, Isabella, was already animatedly sharing a story from her sophomore year, but it was his nephew, Nicholas, who immediately locked eyes with him.

At twenty-two, Nicholas sat with a certain poised intensity that Michael recognized all too well—it was the same hunger he had felt at that age, a restlessness that even the comforts of a Sunday dinner couldn't quite soothe.

Nicholas spotted Michael first and stood to greet him. "Uncle Michael, I've been meaning to call you," he said, pulling him into a quick hug. "I drove past the Harbor Point site yesterday. The way you repositioned that property is brilliant. Everyone in my development class at Miami Herbert used it as an example of turning dead retail into mixed-use gold."

Michael laughed as he shrugged off his jacket. "You mean the class where you argued with your professor about cap rates?"

Nicholas grinned. "He was wrong. And you proved it."

Even now, Nicholas talked about properties the way other guys his age talked about cars or sports—analyzing layouts, foot traffic, zoning angles. Michael had seen that spark long before business school ever refined it. During summers and holiday breaks, Nicholas had practically lived at Stratus Meridian Group's offices, tagging along to site visits, asking questions contractors rarely expected from a teenager, absorbing everything he could about deals, design, and negotiations.

Michael pulled out a chair, a small, knowing smile tugging at his mouth. Being only eleven years older than Nicholas, the two had always shared a bond that felt more like a brotherhood than a traditional uncle-nephew relationship.

While Anthony and Michael had been the ones to lay the foundation of Stratus Meridian Group, Nicholas had been their most devoted shadow, spending every school vacation and long weekend immersed in the grit of the real estate world. He hadn't just studied the industry from a textbook at Miami Herbert; he had breathed it in on construction sites and in high-stakes boardrooms.

Michael had watched him, seeing the way Nicholas's gaze scanned the room with a developer's eye, already calculating the potential in every square inch. While Nicholas was certainly an asset to the family firm now, Michael saw a fire in his eyes that suggested he wasn't content to remain a shadow. He had the distinct feeling that Nicholas was destined for a path he would carve out entirely on his own.

Vincent had opened a wonderful magnum of red Grand Cru Burgundy, pouring glasses for himself, Cheryl, Nick, and Nicholas, while Bev, Isabella, and Angela sipped champagne. Their father, Dominic, stayed away from alcohol these days—doctor's orders, with his sugar levels climbing.

"So, what happened to you last night?" Bev asked as Michael slid into his chair, her sharp eyes locking onto him.

Michael smirked, reaching for a glass of wine. "I made my appearance."

"I saw you dancing awfully close with Thessaly's friend Verónica," Bev pressed, her tone laced with knowing curiosity. "Did she take up all your time?"

Michael shrugged casually. "We talked for a little while before she went home."

Vincent leaned in with a grin, his voice teasing. "And exactly how did she get home?"

Michael gave a mock sigh. "I guess it's interrogate-Michael day."

Laughter rippled around the table, but Bev wasn't done. She set her glass down with a soft clink. "Go easy with Verónica, Michael. She just went through a tough divorce. She's not one of your playthings."

Michael arched a brow, his smile never fading. "So that's what you think of me, sis?"

"I think," Bev said, leaning back with a smirk, "that you change women like I change my dresses. You're my baby brother, and I love you, but I know your MO."

The table erupted again in laughter. Anthony raised his glass. "Here comes the prosecutor."

Bev rolled her eyes, but her grin betrayed her amusement. "You all love it when I give Michael a hard time. Admit it."

Vincent lifted his glass higher. "This calls for more wine!"

The chuckling deepened, filling the house with warmth. But later, when the noise had quieted, Bev pulled Michael aside.

"I don't know if you know this," she began softly, "but Verónica started a new job after her divorce. It hasn't been easy for her. She's drowning in debt that her ex left her with, and her new firm is pressuring her about billable hours. She's struggling."

Michael nodded slowly. "She mentioned she had started a new job."

"But probably not the rest," Bev said. "I like her, Michael. She's a good person, and she's a brilliant lawyer. She doesn't deserve to lose her footing because of her ex. If you have any contacts who might be able to throw some work her way... maybe give her a shot... I'd appreciate it." She hesitated, then added with a smile, "And for the record, you two looked really cute on the dance floor."

Michael's lips curved into a rare, genuine smile. "Let me think about it. I'll see what I can do. What's her last name?"

"Liora," Bev said, pressing a kiss to his cheek. "I love you, Michael."

"I know," he replied softly. "I love you too, sis."

Michael never breathed a word about Verónica to his siblings beyond that. Odd, considering he normally would have given them at least some hint. Not details, never that—but enough to let them know he had enjoyed someone's company. With Verónica, though, he kept it close, guarded.

The next morning, Michael sat in his office, staring at the massive construction progress board pinned across the wall. Each project stood marked with timelines, notes, and color-coded updates. One in particular caught his attention: Solara Edge. It was to be a seventy-story ultra-luxury residential tower rising in the heart of downtown Miami. The city had already granted approval, and as Michael scanned the board, he saw that groundbreaking was now only a few months away.

Sara, his secretary, entered with her usual efficiency, dropping the morning mail on his desk. "Coffee?" she asked.

"Yes, please. And send Ralph in."

Minutes later, Ralph stepped into the office. "Sara said you wanted me?"

Michael gestured toward the chair. "Sit. What law firm were you thinking of for Solara Edge?"

Ralph shrugged. "We've had Frances & Frances handle the approval process. They did a good job. I figured we'd let them continue—construction contracts, rental agreements, the complete package."

Michael leaned back, tapping his pen against the desk. "How many of our projects are they already working on?"

"Three, including Solara Edge," Ralph answered.

Michael shook his head. "Too many. Let them finish up any revisions on the approvals, but don't give them more of Solara Edge." He paused, then added, "Call Delgado, Mercer & Klein LLP. Ask specifically for Verónica Liora. Tell her you're with Stratus Meridian Group and would like to discuss a potential working relationship. Don't mention my name."

Ralph's brow furrowed. "Can I ask why?"

Michael's tone was smooth, final. "Someone asked me for a favor. And you know I like spreading out the work."

Ralph looked unconvinced but didn't press. "Got it. I'll set up the meeting."

Before Michael left for the day, Ralph tapped on his door to confirm that the call had been made. He had reached out to Delgado, Mercer & Klein, and the meeting with Verónica was officially on the books for Thursday.

Chapter 8

Verónica

She couldn't stop thinking about Michael—how he made her feel, how his touch had branded itself into her skin. No matter how hard she tried, she couldn't push away the memory of his hands, his mouth, his body pressed against hers, his manhood deep inside her, touching places she never knew existed. Every detail replayed itself in her mind like a film she couldn't pause. The more days that passed without him, the fainter her hope of ever seeing him again became. Yet his memory remained as vivid as if it were yesterday, scorching and impossible to shake.

Late Monday morning, as Verónica worked at her desk drafting a contract, the receptionist's voice came through as she answered the office phone. "Ms. Liora, I have a Ralph Murphy from Stratus Meridian Group on the phone for you."

She frowned, pen pausing in her hand. Ralph Murphy? Stratus Meridian Group? She had never heard of either. Probably a sales call or a bill collector from Gregory's debts, she thought. Still, her bosses had been on her about missing opportunities. If it turned out to be nonsense, she could cut him off quickly. "Put him through," she said, trying to keep her voice even.

"Hi, Verónica. I'm Ralph Murphy, Sr. VP with Stratus Meridian Group. Have you heard of us?"

"I'm sorry, I haven't," she replied, already bracing herself to hang up. "How can I help you?"

"Well, we're one of the largest commercial builders in South Florida," he said smoothly. "I was wondering if you'd be open to a meeting to discuss possibly taking us on as a new client."

Verónica nearly dropped the phone. A new client? Not just any client—but one of the biggest developers in the region? Her pulse spiked. "Yes, I—I would be very interested," she stammered. "How about Thursday at eleven AM here at the office?"

"Perfect," Ralph replied. "I'll see you Thursday."

She hung up the phone, heart pounding, and immediately pulled up her browser. One search, and her breath caught. There, splashed across Stratus Meridian Group's homepage, was a glossy photograph of Michael Marino standing proudly in front of one of his newly completed towers, Harbor Point, with his brother Anthony beside him. The very building he had taken her to that unforgettable night.

Shock rippled through her. Michael. Her throat tightened. Was this meeting happening because he pitied her? Because he had missed her? Or was this just a coincidence? The thought of him alone was enough to stir heat between her thighs; her body betraying her all over again.

The door creaked, and Peter, one of the firm's partners, walked into her office. His tone was sharp. "Verónica, I think we need to talk."

Her mind raced. "Okay, but—before we do—are you available Thursday at eleven?"

Peter blinked. "Verónica, Thursday morning, we have a general office meeting at ten-thirty. Did you forget?"

"Oh my God," she breathed. Panic set in. "I just committed to a meeting with Stratus Meridian Group."

Peter froze. "What? With who? How?"

She explained quickly. She had received a call out of the blue from Ralph Murphy, who said he wanted to discuss the possibility of our firm working for Stratus Meridian Group. To her surprise, Peter's entire face transformed. His eyes widened, a frantic kind of energy taking over his features as he began to pace the small office. "I've been trying to get a meeting with Michael Marino for months. He always blows me off and never makes time for me. This... this is huge." He paced, muttering under his breath, then looked at her firmly. "You keep that meeting. I'll reschedule the office meeting. And yes, I will make myself available. This could be the most important thing we land this year."

Verónica sat, stunned. "What did you want to talk to me about, then?"

Peter waved a hand dismissively. "Nothing important. Forget it."

In that instant, she realized the truth: Michael had just saved her job. But why?

When Thursday morning arrived, Verónica chose her best dress, the one that hugged her figure without being too much. Matching heels, polished hair, and understated jewelry. She looked in the mirror and told herself she looked as good as she could. She didn't know if Michael would actually be there—but God, she hoped.

At 10:45 am, she and Peter waited in the conference room, nerves and anticipation coiling tight in her chest. By eleven sharp, the door opened. Ralph entered with a tall man and a strikingly beautiful woman at his side.

The woman was flawless—long legs, sleek black hair, and an expensive, fitted suit that screamed confidence.

Ralph introduced his colleagues. "This is Javier, my assistant. He makes sure all the projects I oversee run smoothly."

The man nodded politely, then sat back as the woman smiled. "And I'm María, VP of Projects. I work directly with Michael, the president of the real estate division. I liaise with all the project directors and update Michael daily."

The words hit like a punch. Directly with Michael. Daily. Verónica felt the blood rush to her face, her jealousy ballooning into something almost unbearable. Her stomach knotted instantly. Did he touch her as he touched me? Did she moan for him the way I did? The insecurity clawed at her until she silently scolded herself. Stop it. Focus. This is business.

María's gaze seemed to weigh heavily on Verónica, staying a beat longer than was comfortable. When she spoke, her voice had a sharp, polished quality that felt to Verónica like a hidden challenge. "Michael usually prefers working with experienced attorneys on contracts. Do you have much experience with commercial construction contracts, Ms. Liora?"

Verónica clenched her hands under the table, her nails digging into her palms. I swear I'll scratch your perfect little eyes out.

Before she could answer, Ralph cut in smoothly. "I'll handle this. Verónica, I'd like you to put together a proposal with your rates and the number of attorneys and paralegals you can allocate to our account. I should warn you—Mr. Marino is very demanding. Do you think you're up to it?"

She sat straighter, forcing her voice to remain steady, though her heart hammered. "Yes," she said, her chin lifting. "I can definitely handle it. And I'm confident Mr. Marino will be satisfied with the quality of work this firm produces."

Ralph's lips curved into what looked like a smile of approval. "Good. I look forward to your proposal."

They all stood, shook hands, exchanged polite goodbyes, and then the group was gone.

The second they were back in her office, Peter was practically glowing. He looked as if he'd just won the lottery. "I don't know how you did that, but it was a lifeline. You were excellent in there."

Verónica managed a smile. "Thank you."

But the second the door closed, her bravado crumbled. All she could think about was Michael. That night at the wedding, when he had saved her from despair, when he had unlocked a side of her she didn't know existed. And today—without even showing his face—he had saved her career.

Why won't he call me? The question gnawed at her. Why won't he touch me again? Hold me again? Every part of her ached for him. Should she call and thank him? No—she couldn't. Thessaly wouldn't. Susan wouldn't. But then again, they hadn't been the ones in his arms that night. They hadn't felt what she had felt.

That night, Verónica sat curled on her bed, the city lights bleeding through her curtains. Her laptop sat closed on the desk, the draft of her proposal untouched. She should have been working, but instead she was caught in the loop of his face, his voice, his hands.

Everywhere she turned, Michael was there. In the rustle of sheets when she lay down, she felt again the weight of his body pressing hers into the mattress. In the faint trace of cologne that lingered in her memory, her skin tingled as if his lips had just brushed her neck. Her body remembered him in ways her heart didn't want to admit.

Her phone sat on the nightstand, silent. She picked it up more than once, thumb hovering over her contacts, tempted to call Thessaly for advice, or Beverly for Michael's number, so she could be tempted even more to text him. Just a thank you, she told herself. Nothing more. Just gratitude.

But then her pride surged. What if he hadn't been thinking of her at all? What if giving her this opportunity was nothing more than a business move, a detached favor for his cousin's friend? To call him would be to expose her longing, to hand him power over her heart.

She tossed the phone back down, pressed the heels of her hands to her eyes, and groaned. "God, why can't I just forget him?" She whispered to the empty room.

Sleep came late, and when it did, it betrayed her. She dreamed of him—Michael's mouth trailing fire down her skin, his voice murmuring her name, his arms locking her against him like he never wanted to let go. She woke with her pulse racing, her body aching, the sheets twisted around her legs like a lover's embrace.

She hated herself for it. Hated the weakness, the craving, the way one man had unraveled her so completely. And yet... she couldn't help it.

Maybe Thessaly and Susan would never call him. But Verónica wasn't Thessaly. She wasn't Susan. She was herself—caught between fear and desire, shame and hope. And as the night stretched on, one truth burned clear in her chest: she wanted him again. No matter how much she tried to convince herself otherwise, she wanted him.

Chapter 9

Michael

Michael woke before dawn, the Miami skyline painted in deep blues and pale grays outside his window. He lay still, staring at the ceiling, but his mind wasn't quiet. It hadn't been quiet since the wedding.

He had tried to shake her, tried to lose her in the noise of work, in the endless parade of deals and contracts and polished faces that wanted something from him. But Verónica lingered like an echo in his chest. Her voice, soft yet sharp; her eyes when they had locked with his on the dance floor; her body trembling beneath his touch—every detail haunted him.

It frustrated him more than he wanted to admit. Women had come and gone, some remembered, most forgotten. That was how he lived—keep it light, keep it simple, never let it dig too deep. But with her, it had been different. The memory of her wasn't fading. If anything, it was sharpening.

He rolled onto his side, raking a hand through his hair. Why her? Why now? She wasn't supposed to matter. She deserved more than what he was willing—or able—to give. Relationships had never fit into his life. They tangled; they demanded. They slowed him down. And yet, for the first time in years, he wondered what it might be like not to be alone.

He cursed softly under his breath and pushed himself out of bed. He wouldn't go there. He couldn't. Not with her. Not when she had that fragile look in her eyes, that rawness from a man who had broken her down piece by piece. He told himself he wasn't her savior. He wasn't her future.

Still, as he buttoned his shirt and reached for his Rolex watch, he caught his reflection in the mirror and admitted the truth he didn't want to face: he wanted her again. Badly. More than he should.

Michael straightened his tie, set his jaw, and grabbed his briefcase. If he buried himself deep enough at work, maybe the thoughts of Verónica would fade. At least, that's what he told himself as he walked out the door.

Michael reached the office earlier than usual; he had skipped the gym, too restless to focus on the rhythm of weights or the repetition of his routine. Instead, he was determined to drown his thoughts in the only thing that had ever steadied him—contracts, figures, and the cold clarity of numbers. Yet even as he spread the files across his desk, her face lingered in his mind. Verónica. The curve of her smile, the fire in her eyes, the way her body had trembled under his hands. No spreadsheet or proposal could smother the memory. No calculation could quiet the hunger she had awakened inside him.

He was buried deep in numbers when Ralph stepped into his office carrying a folder. "I have the proposal from Delgado, Mercer & Klein. Would you like to see it, or should Andrea handle it?"

Michael didn't look up right away. Normally, he would have let their in-house counsel, Andrea, handle it, but something tugged at him. "Sure, let me see it."

He flipped through the proposal, scanning the neat columns and summaries. "Rates seem reasonable to me. What did you think of their legal team?"

Ralph chuckled. "Well, Verónica Liora—she'll be our point of contact. With a big smile, she's definitely something to look at, that's for sure. Sexy, classy, and sweet as anyone I've ever seen."

The words landed like sparks against dry timber. Michael felt a rush of heat—an emotion he almost never allowed himself to feel. Jealousy. It tightened in his chest like a vise. He leaned back in his chair, expression calm, detached, but his pulse hammered. "Verónica Liora," he repeated evenly, as if testing the sound. "Good. Let's see what she can do."

Ralph continued, oblivious. "She hasn't had much experience with construction contracts, but she's sharp. Her boss, Peter—I checked,

he's top-notch. He's handled plenty of real estate construction contracts for major firms."

"Fine," Michael said. "Give it to Andrea. Tell her I said it looks good.
She'll execute it."

As Ralph walked out with the papers, Michael sat back in silence.
He hated his insides twisting simply because someone else had noticed what he already knew—how stunning Verónica was. A faint
smile touched his lips. Yes, Ralph was right about one thing. Verónica
was unforgettable.

The following Wednesday, around eleven, Michael sat at his desk
reviewing projections when the closed-circuit monitor caught his
eye. A group of visitors walked past the reception area, but it wasn't
the men who froze him. It was her.

Verónica.

She wore a fitted black skirt that hugged every curve, the hem
brushing just above her knees. Her heels clicked softly against the
marble floor, elegant and confident, yet Michael noticed the faint
tension in her posture. A white blouse clung to her in just the right
places, hinting at the perfection beneath. She shook Ralph's hand,
smiling politely, then followed him toward the conference room.
Javier and María trailed behind.

Michael dropped his pen. For a long moment, he simply stared at
the monitor, torn between restraint and need. Finally, he straightened his tie, rose from his chair, and gave in to the temptation he
could no longer deny.

When he opened the conference room door, every head turned.
Verónica's eyes lifted, and in that instant, the air thickened. Their
gazes locked. Neither smiled. Neither looked away.

Ralph sat at the head of the long conference table with Verónica
to his left, facing the open door, looking poised and professional,
though Michael caught the subtle flicker of nerves in the way she
smoothed her skirt, pressed her lips together, and straightened her
back a little too carefully. Desire coiled in his chest, sharp and dangerous.

Ralph cleared his throat. "Michael—I didn't expect you."

"I thought I'd see for myself who we might be working with," Michael replied, voice steady, betraying nothing. He extended his hand across the table. "Ms. Liora."

Her fingers slid into his—soft, warm, trembling slightly. "Mr. Marino," she said, her voice tight with control, though the fire in her eyes betrayed her composure.

And in that single moment, Michael knew. No contract, no tower, no distraction would ever erase her.

"I'll let you get back to your meeting," he said smoothly. Then his gaze lingered, deliberately softening. "But Ms. Liora—or Verónica, if I may—I understand you're acquainted with my sister, Beverly."

The sudden heat in her cheeks didn't escape him. She seemed to take a bracing breath, trying to smooth over the moment with a calm she obviously didn't feel. 'Yes,' she replied, her gaze flickering to his for only a second. 'Through your cousin, Thessaly.

"Small world," Michael murmured. He let the silence stretch just long enough for her to feel it before adding, "When you're finished with the meeting, stop by my office before you leave."

Michael noticed the shock flicker in her eyes, which she quickly tried to mask. She nodded once. "Certainly."

Michael offered a small, knowing nod before turning to the door. He caught one last glimpse of Verónica—pale, shimmering with a sudden, nervous energy that seemed to pull the air right out of the room. He slipped away, leaving her to the drone of the meeting, well aware that his request had just become the only thing she would be able to hear for the rest of the meeting.

Michael watched the security feed as the meeting ended. He noticed María lean in; her smile forced. "Ms. Liora, would you like me to show you to Michael's office?" Her voice sounded thin and sharp over the speakers, edged with jealousy. Michael saw Verónica stiffen. She felt the sting.

He watched them walk through the sleek hallways. María led the way, stern and unwelcoming. When they reached Sara's desk, she said, "Michael wants to see Ms. Liora." Her tone was curt and cold.

Sara picked up the phone. "Ms. Liora is here." She stood up, opened Michael's door, and motioned for them to come in.

Michael looked up, his gaze sweeping over both women. "Thank you, María."

The dismissal was smooth, absolute. María faltered, then forced a smile. "Of course." She closed the door behind her.

She froze. Right in the doorway.

Michael watched her chest hitch with shallow, panicked breaths. She was trying to keep it together, but he could see the pulse thumping in the hollow of her throat. She looked like a trapped bird in a silk suit.

Michael stood up from behind the polished mahogany desk. His silhouette was framed by the sprawling Miami skyline. He locked eyes with her, and the intensity made her skin prickle.

"How was your meeting?" he asked. His voice was a low, smooth vibration that seemed to travel through the marble floor and straight into the soles of her heels.

Verónica forced her lips into a semblance of a smile, though her fingers were trembling against the leather of her folder. "Good... I hope," she said, the words feeling brittle and inadequate in the heavy silence of the room.

Michael's expression didn't soften; instead, a slow, knowing shadow of a grin tugged at the corner of his mouth. "I'm sure it was," he replied, his tone suggesting he was evaluating a very different kind of performance. He finally stepped out from behind the desk. He moved toward her with a gait that was agonizingly slow—each step deliberate, measured, and undeniably predatory. He was closing the distance, not like a colleague, but like a man reclaiming something he already owned.

The closer he drew, the more the room seemed to shrink, until the only things left in existence were the scent of his expensive cologne and the heat radiating from his frame. As he breached her personal space, the heavy folder she had been clutching like a shield finally betrayed her. Her grip failed, and the documents slipped from her numb fingers, landing on the side table where she stood with a soft, muffled thud. The sound felt final, like a gavel coming down, signaling the end of her professional defenses and the beginning of whatever he had planned next.

"Tell me to stop," he murmured, his hand sliding firmly against her waist, pulling her toward him. The heat in his grip betrayed the hunger burning inside him.

Her lips parted, but no words came. The silence was her answer.

His mouth captured hers in a kiss that stole the air from her lungs—hungry, searing, everything she had been starving for since the wedding night. She melted into him, her hands clutching his chest, his shoulders, the back of his neck, pulling him closer as if terrified he might vanish.

Michael pressed her against the far wall of the office, the cool surface biting into her back, a sharp contrast to the inferno between them. His hands roamed urgently, memorizing her all over again. Her gasp broke against his mouth—a sound of both surrender and need.

"This is wrong," she whispered, though her arms locked tighter around him.

"Maybe," he rasped against her throat, his lips trailing fire down her skin. "But it doesn't feel wrong."

Every warning in her mind screamed, but her body betrayed her. Her fingers tangled in his hair, her mouth found his again, and in that moment, she stopped caring.

Outside the door, the office buzzed with business, but inside Michael's office, the world narrowed to heat, hunger, and reckless need. Verónica no longer cared who she was supposed to be—only that she was his, if only for this stolen moment.

Michael's mouth ravaged hers, each kiss deeper, more desperate than the last. Verónica's body arched against him, every nerve alight. His hands slid down her sides, gripping her hips, pulling her flush against the hard lines of his body. The evidence of his desire pressed into her, making her moan softly into his mouth.

"Oh, my God..." she gasped when his lips trailed along her jaw, down the column of her throat. Her head fell back against the wall, surrendering to his hunger.

He nipped at her skin, his breath hot and ragged. "I've tried to forget you," he growled against her pulse, "but you're under my skin, Verónica. I can't." His words broke off as his lips crashed back to hers, devouring her with a hunger that shook them both.

Verónica's hands were a blur of motion, tugging at his shirt until the buttons gave way. When she finally pressed her hands to his skin, her palms were searing. Michael could feel the raw urgency in her grip, a demand for more that matched the fire in his own blood. It felt as though she couldn't get close enough; her every movement an effort to strip away the world until it was just skin on skin.

Michael's hands tangled in her hair, tilting her face up to his as the kiss deepened. Frantic, dangerous. His other hand skimmed lower, gripping her thigh, hitching her leg slightly up against him. The movement made her whimper—a sound that sent fire straight through him.

He pressed harder, pinning her to the wall, every inch of him demanding, claiming. For a wild, breathless moment, nothing else existed but the heat, the hunger, the raw need threatening to consume them both.

His hand slid beneath her skirt, fingertips grazing the silk of her thong, feeling her soaked womanhood. Her body shivered at his touch, a strangled moan slipping out as his fingers found her slick heat. Pushing the fabric aside, he stroked her sweet spot, slow at first, teasing, then firmer as her hips moved helplessly against him.

Her moans grew louder, broken, pleading. "Please don't stop, Michael... don't stop."

He slipped a finger inside her, then another, his thumb circling her swollen nub with ruthless precision. Verónica buried her face against his neck, muffling her cries as the climax built, fierce and unstoppable. She clung to him; her nails digging into his skin, then bit softly against his chest to silence the scream that tore through her as her body shattered.

Michael held her close, feeling her tremble, her legs weak. He worked her through a second wave and then slowly eased his fingers from her, then lifted them to his mouth, tasting her. His eyes locked onto hers. "You taste amazing," he murmured, raw heat in his voice.

Verónica's mouth slammed into his, her kiss deep and insatiable. Michael felt the sudden shift in her—as if the taste of herself on his lips had only poured gasoline on her fire, driving her to press even harder against him.

Michael broke the kiss with effort, his forehead pressed against hers. "God, I want you now. But if we finish this here..." His voice was hoarse, strained. "...we'll never walk out of this office without everyone knowing."

Her lips trembled against his, still burning, still desperate. "Michael..." she whispered, her voice thick with longing.

He pulled her tighter, then exhaled a ragged breath. "This is hard enough."

He felt her slump against him, a silent admission that he was right. He could see the same agonizing pull in her eyes that he felt in his own chest—a shared realization that if they let go now, there would be no stopping. And an office in the middle of the day, with the world just outside the door, wasn't where he wanted them to burn.

She swallowed hard, her chest rising and falling in a jagged rhythm as she fought for breath. "Then when?" she asked, her lips brushing his. The question came out like a confession, soft and broken.

Michael's jaw clenched, his eyes dark with a need that felt like an anchor dragging him down. He pulled back just far enough to see her, his thumb brushing her cheek—a tender gesture that felt at odds with the raw hunger still humming between them. "I'm not what you need, Verónica. You're perfection. You deserve someone who can give you this... every hour, every day. I can't."

He felt a tremor run through her entire body at his words. She gave a small, jerky nod, her eyes searching for a composure she clearly hadn't found. "Then I'll wait," she whispered. The words hung in the air, heavy with an ache that Michael felt deep in his own bones.

She turned away to his private bathroom to fix her makeup, leaving him alone in the sudden silence of the office. Michael straightened his own shirt, his hands slightly unsteady as he tried to mask the storm he knew was still visible in his eyes. When she emerged, she looked composed to the world, but he noticed the slight lingering shine in her eyes and the way she wouldn't quite meet his gaze.

Before she reached the door, he pulled her into one last embrace. He held her as if it might be the last time he'd ever feel her against him. She clung to his shoulders, her fingers digging into his jacket with a desperate reluctance that matched the tightening of his own arms.

Finally, he forced himself to step back. The loss of her touch felt like a tearing wound. The silence stretched between them, heavy and dangerous, the air still thick with everything they had almost surrendered to.

His voice was low, steady, but edged with fire. "Go. Before I forget myself completely."

Her lips, swollen from his kisses, trembled. She nodded, gathering her things with movements that seemed stiff, almost forced. He watched her walk toward the door, every step looking like a battle. She didn't look back—and Michael knew that if she did, he wouldn't have the strength to let her leave a second time.

Chapter 10

Verónica

As Verónica left Michael's office, she forced a polite smile and murmured a soft goodbye to Sara, praying his assistant couldn't see how badly her composure was slipping. The warmth of Michael's hands still clung to her skin, and the memory of his kiss lingered on her lips as if it had happened seconds ago.

She stepped into the elevator and pressed the lobby button. The doors slid shut with a muted hiss, cutting her off from the hallway—and from him. As the car began its slow descent, her stomach dropped with it. Each passing floor felt like another layer of certainty falling away, the quiet hum of the cables overhead echoing the tight, hollow feeling forming in her chest.

By the time the elevator passed the twentieth floor, tears blurred her vision. She leaned back against the cold metal wall; the chill seeping through her blouse as she bit down on her lip to keep the first sob from escaping. The faint scent of polished steel and cool air wrapped around her, sterile and unforgiving, nothing like the warmth she had just left behind. All she wanted was to go home, curl up in her bed, and cry until the ache loosening inside her finally emptied itself out.

But the elevator kept descending, steady and indifferent, reminding her that the day wasn't over. Contracts still waited on her desk. Deadlines didn't care about rejection, longing, or disappointment. When the doors opened, she would have to step out, wipe her face, return to her office, and prove—once again—that she belonged on the Solara Edge project.

Michael might have broken her heart, holding her close only to remind her he couldn't give her the forever she craved, but she refused to let that destroy her. She would pour every ounce of herself into this job, deliver a flawless performance, and make Stratus Meridian Group see her value. Maybe then, maybe someday, Michael would finally understand what she truly was to him.

Later that night, exhaustion clung to her as she sat curled on her couch, papers spread across the coffee table. She had pushed through hours of work, forcing herself to focus on contracts and clauses, but now that the house was quiet, her defenses collapsed. A half-empty glass of wine dangled from her fingers, its warmth doing little to numb the hollow ache inside her chest. She closed her eyes, but that only made the memories sharper—the way Michael had kissed her as though he couldn't breathe without her, the way his hands had claimed her, the way his fingers had brought her to ecstasy against his office wall.

She shuddered, pressing her palm against her lips as if she could trap the taste of him there. How complete she had felt in his arms, how undeniable the connection had been. How could he not see it? How could he pretend it wasn't real? To her, it seemed his composure had finally fractured; she had heard his voice catch with a raw, unvarnished need and seen a fire in his eyes that she was certain mirrored the one consuming her. He wanted her—the realization hummed in her blood—she was convinced he wanted her as desperately as she wanted him.

Then why did he push her away? Was she not enough for him? The cruel thought twisted through her heart like a blade, dragging her back to Gregory's voice, Gregory's taunts, the lies he had whispered that had left scars still unhealed.

Her phone chimed, startling her from the spiral of pain. She glanced at the screen—Susan. With a heavy sigh, she forced cheer into her voice and answered. "Hello."

"Verónica!" Susan practically yelled, her tone bubbling with energy. "How's my girl doing?"

"I'm good," she lied, her voice soft, fragile.

"No, you're not," Susan shot back instantly. "Don't even try it. I can hear it. Tell me what's going on. Is it Gregory again?"

Verónica's chest tightened. "No. It's not him."

"Then who?" Susan demanded. "Talk to me."

"It's... It's such a long story. I can't right now," Verónica said quickly, her throat tightening around the words. "I promise I'll tell you when we're together."

Susan sighed heavily, but let it go for now.

They continued talking about other things, finally circling back to Susan's ever-colorful love life. Susan gushed about the new man she had dated—how he was well-off, spoiled her with dinners at the best restaurants, drove a shiny new Porsche, and surprised her with little gifts for no reason at all. "He's not the best in the bedroom," Susan admitted with a laugh, "but he makes up for it in other areas. He even picked up the phone and set up a new account for me. It could be huge for me. His bedroom skills may be lacking behind closed doors, but as long as the contracts keep coming, I'm not complaining."

Verónica smiled politely, making small noises of acknowledgment, but inside her chest tightened. Her mind wasn't on Susan's Porsche-driving suitor or his lackluster bedroom skills. It was on Michael—always Michael.

Perfect in ways that Susan's new man could never measure up to. Perfect in the way his hands could undo her with a single touch—the way his kiss consumed her, left her trembling, desperate, alive. He was fire and danger and safety all at once, and the memory of him lingered like a secret she carried everywhere.

She wanted to tell Susan. To blurt it out, to confess that she had found a man who made her feel whole, who had awakened something inside her she never knew existed. But she bit her tongue. She couldn't. Not now. Maybe never. The risk was too great—for her job, for her heart.

Instead, she listened in silence, her thoughts miles away, her heart aching with a longing she couldn't put into words. By the time they said their goodbyes and promised to talk soon, Verónica set her phone down and exhaled slowly, as if she'd been holding her breath throughout the entire conversation. She closed her eyes, whispering his name in the quiet of her apartment, a name she could never share out loud. No one could know about Michael. Not about the wedding night. Not about the fire in his office today. If word ever got out, she could lose everything—her reputation, her career, the biggest account she had just landed.

So she would keep her secret. She would bury the truth beneath contracts and long hours and quiet, wine-filled nights. But deep inside, she wished she could scream it to the world, wished she could tell someone what it felt like to be wanted by Michael Marino. Maybe then, just maybe, the ache of his rejection wouldn't feel so unbearable.

Chapter 11
Michael

Michael sat frozen behind his desk long after the door had clicked shut, the faint trace of her perfume still clinging to the air. His pulse intensified, his body tense, every nerve alight from the memory of her lips and the feel of her trembling in his arms. He dragged a hand across his face, cursing under his breath.

What the hell was he doing? He had let himself lose control—again. He had promised himself after the wedding night that it was over, that she was better off without him. Yet the second he had seen her walk into his building, polished, beautiful, determined—he had been undone. The careful distance he had built crumbled in an instant.

He leaned back in his chair, staring at the ceiling, jaw tight. He should never have touched her. She should have remained professional and untouchable, just another attorney trying to earn his business. But the moment their eyes met in the conference room, he couldn't help himself.

Verónica Liora. She haunted him. No number on his desk, no contract in his hand, could erase the image of her lips parting for him, the sound of her moans in his ear. He had taken risks before—business, family, even his own life—but this was different. She wasn't just a temptation. She was dangerous—not for who she was, but for how she made him feel.

His thoughts tangled with guilt and desire. He could hear her voice cracking when she whispered his name, the way her body clung to his as if she couldn't let go. God help him, he hadn't wanted her to. He had wanted to strip her bare, take her against the wall, lose himself inside her until nothing else mattered. Only sheer willpower—and the walls around his office—had stopped him.

He pressed his fists against the desk, head bowed. He had to let her go. She deserved more than stolen moments in his office, more than a man who could never promise her anything beyond now. And yet... the thought of never touching her again felt suffocating.

Michael's eyes flicked toward the closed door, as if she still stood there, flushed, trembling, lips swollen from his kiss. His chest ached with a strange, unfamiliar longing—not just lust, not just hunger, but something deeper, something far more dangerous.

With a growl, he stood and poured himself a drink; the amber liquid burned down his throat. He told himself he was in control, that this ended here. But deep down, he knew the truth: this wasn't the end. It was only the beginning.

That evening, Olivia called, her voice soft but uncertain. "Michael, do you want to get together? It feels like forever since I've seen you—since before the wedding."

He pinched the bridge of his nose, staring at the stack of proposals for the Solara Edge project. "I can't tonight," he said, tone clipped. "I'm buried in contracts."

She hesitated, then finally asked the question that was on her mind, her voice sounding small and strained. "Are you...upset with me? For getting sick and not going to the wedding with you?"

Michael's chest tightened. He thought of telling her the truth—that the only thing weighing on his mind was a woman named Verónica. But instead, he sighed. "Of course not, Olivia. I just have a lot going on. I'll call you next week."

He heard the unmistakable weight of disappointment in her voice before she wished him goodnight and hung up. He tossed the phone onto his desk, running a hand through his hair. Olivia didn't even factor into his thoughts anymore. Every corner of his mind belonged to Verónica, and it was slowly driving him crazy.

By Friday night, Michael gave up fighting the restlessness and went out for a drink at one of Miami's downtown hot spots. The lounge throbbed with restrained luxury, a place where the lighting was soft, the music low, and temptation hung in the air like an expensive perfume. He sat at the bar with a Bivi Martini—iced, lemon peel, two olives—hoping the burn would dull his thoughts. But as he lifted the glass, his mind betrayed him again, replaying the memory of Verónica's lips, her scent clinging to his skin, the way her body trembled against his.

"Jeez," he muttered under his breath. "She's going to be my downfall." He tried to shake it, told himself the truth he had always lived by: You don't do relationships, Michael. You never have. You're not ready, and probably never will be.

A beautiful woman approached—long legs, a rose-colored silk blouse, eyes sparkling with interest. Gorgeous figure. "I see you're sitting alone," she said, tilting her head toward the dance floor. "This is my favorite song. Would you like to dance?"

He turned, letting his eyes sweep over her with automatic appreciation. Any other night, he would have smiled, taken her hand, and let the evening play out exactly as she invited. But tonight? He shook his head. "Not tonight."

Surprise flickered across her face before she moved on. Michael turned back to his drink, scowling. What the hell was wrong with him? Beautiful women, casual encounters, no strings—that was his life. And yet he couldn't bring himself to touch anyone else. He tossed back the rest of his martini, pushed away from the bar, and left.

Later, lying in bed, he stared at the ceiling, imagining Verónica beside him—the sound of her laugh, the fire of her kiss, the way she whispered his name. His body ached for her, but his mind wouldn't let him reach out.

Instead, it dragged him back seven years, to Cathy—the last woman who had meant anything. She had been his first actual girlfriend since his teenage years. Beautiful, magnetic, the woman who turned heads just as he did. When they walked into a room, people stared. For a while, it was intoxicating.

The passion between them had burned hot, relentless, almost too much. But as the months wore on, Michael realized it was all they had. Cathy loved horror flicks; he preferred thrillers with substance. She blasted the latest pop hits; he savored oldies like Sinatra, Motown, and Whitney Houston. She was content with greasy hot dogs on the boardwalk; he craved fine cuisine, the subtle artistry of sushi, and the richness of French dining. The cracks widened, and one day he woke up knowing that the only thing binding them together was sex.

It had been wild, raw, but empty. Not like Verónica. With her, it wasn't just lust—it was a connection. Fire that reached his bones stripped him bare, leaving him craving not just her body, but her soul.

When Cathy was gone, Michael swore off relationships forever. And yet here he was, caught in a loop of thoughts about a woman who had slipped past every defense he'd built. He wanted her in every part of his life, but knew he couldn't allow it.

Saturday came and went in a haze. He barely got out of bed, depression sinking in like a sickness. By nightfall, he sat with a bottle of vodka and a half-watched movie, Verónica's face flashing through his mind in every shadow, every silence.

By Sunday morning, he forced himself to shower, put on a clean shirt, and head to his father's house for their usual family dinner. The familiar warmth of home should have settled him, but his mind was elsewhere.

As they passed plates of food around the table, Beverly looked up. "Did you get the invitation for Aunt Dolly's fortieth anniversary celebration?"

Michael shook his head. "No. When is it?"

"Two months from now. And you know Aunt Dolly—everything she does has to be a spectacle." Beverly smirked. "Better tell Olivia not to get sick this time."

He arched an eyebrow. "And what makes you think I'm bringing Olivia?"

"Because she's been your stand-in at family functions lately," Beverly teased. "Unless..." She narrowed her eyes, a knowing glint sparking. "There's someone else you're planning to bring?"

Michael leaned back in his chair, masking the flicker of heat that rushed through him at the thought. "I haven't decided yet. I'll give it some thought."

But deep down, the truth was already clear. The only person he wanted on his arm, the only woman he wanted the world to see at his side... was Verónica.

Chapter 12

Verónica

On Monday morning, Verónica arrived at her office early, ready to focus on the Solara Edge construction contracts. The weekend had been rough. Michael was on her mind constantly, even in her dreams, where she could still feel his kiss and his touch. She kept replaying that hour in his office, every detail stuck in her memory. As she organized her files, she told herself it was time to move on. If he didn't want her, she needed to find the strength to let go.

Her heart wanted something else, but her mind held on to work as her only escape. She decided to throw herself into her job, hoping that busy days and tight deadlines would help her forget the pain. If Michael couldn't give her what she needed, she would find purpose in her work. Solara Edge would be her focus, her shield, and her way to cope.

She dove in quickly, working closely with Ralph on contract details. He was kind, respectful, and always steady when he spoke with her. She spoke to him two, sometimes three times a week, and though it was strictly professional, there was a comfort in his easy manner. One week, Peter joined them in her office for a scheduled meeting.

When Ralph arrived, Verónica was surprised to see María with him. They met in the conference room, and though María had no direct role in contracts, she seemed intent on inserting herself into the conversation. Verónica felt the familiar chill as María looked her way, ignoring Verónica's attempted handshake and slipping in little digs, each carrying the unspoken message that María was closer to Michael, more important than Verónica would ever be.

Verónica wasn't sure if anything had ever happened between Michael and María, or if María simply carried a torch for him. Either way, the hostility was clear. Still, Verónica kept her composure, refusing to give María the satisfaction of a reaction.

After the meeting, Peter left, and María went to the ladies' room, leaving Verónica alone with Ralph. Ralph paused, then quietly said, "I probably shouldn't say this. It's against company policy to mix business with pleasure. But you're beautiful, Verónica. Charming. I'd like to know if you'd have dinner with me sometime."

The words startled her. Ralph was a good man—smart, fairly attractive, genuinely kind—but he wasn't Michael. No one was Michael. "I'm not sure that's a good idea," she said carefully. "As you said, mixing business and pleasure isn't wise. But... let me think about it."

Ralph smiled. "I understand. At least it's not a flat no."

When María returned, her sharp eyes flickered between them, and Verónica wondered if she had overheard. They said their goodbyes, and soon Verónica was back at her desk, staring blankly at her files.

Why couldn't it have been Michael asking her to dinner? Why did Ralph's kind offer feel like salt on an open wound? She sighed, pressing her fingers to her temples. Even if she agreed, even if she allowed herself one night of pleasant company, it could complicate everything—her job, her fragile connection to Michael, her own heart.

That evening, Susan called. The moment Verónica answered, Susan said, "Well, you sound better. Did someone finally make you smile in the bedroom?"

Verónica let out a laugh, shaking her head. "No. I've just been focused on work. Things are going well." She paused, then admitted, "Although today I was a little shocked—someone I'm working with asked me to dinner."

"Ooooh!" Susan teased. "I hope you said yes. Is he cute? Rich?"

"I said I'd think about it. He's cute. Not rich, but comfortable."

"Then go for it, girl! Maybe he could make you scream as he's pumping you full of passion. What have you got to lose?"

"My job," Verónica replied dryly. "Mixing business and pleasure isn't smart."

Susan laughed. "That's so old school—I do it all the time."

Verónica chuckled, shaking her head. "You are so bad, Susan."

After more playful chatter, Susan signed off with, "Keep me posted on your new heartthrob."

When the call ended, Verónica set her phone down and stared at it for a long moment. Heartthrob. If Susan only knew. If she knew the truth—that the only man capable of unraveling her, making her scream sounds of passion, of setting her soul on fire, was the very one she couldn't have.

The following week, an envelope arrived. Verónica opened it and froze. An invitation to the Stratus Meridian Group's tenth anniversary gala, to be held on Saturday, November 1st, at the Four Seasons Miami. Her heart pounded. Who had put her on the list? Was it Ralph? Or—she dared to hope—Michael?

Her thoughts spun wildly. Four weeks. Four weeks to prepare, to buy a dress, to have her hair styled, a manicure, and a pedicure. Four weeks to wonder if this would be the night—the night she could dance with Michael again, feel his hands on her, lose herself in him, just as she had at the wedding. The memory of that dance, of how the night had ended, surged back with a force that left her breathless.

A few days later, after discussing contracts, Ralph asked casually, "I assume you're coming to the gala?"

"Yes," she said. "I was surprised to get an invitation."

Ralph smiled. "We all get to invite people we do business with. Since you still haven't told me when we're having dinner, I figured at least I'd get a dance with you at that gala."

Her stomach dropped. Disappointment pricked at her heart, though she kept her voice light. So it was Ralph who'd added her name. She forced a smile. "That sounds very nice. I look forward to it."

Ralph's smile widened, and Verónica heard an unmistakable heat in his voice. 'Me too,' he said. "I'll talk to you once you finish the next batch of contracts."

When she hung up, Verónica sat back, torn. Maybe she should just give Ralph a chance. He was kind, attentive, and the only one showing her any interest. Maybe she should let herself be seen, admired, and wanted by someone who wasn't afraid to claim her. But still... she couldn't bring herself to commit. Her heart refused to listen to reason. She would wait—at least until after the gala. Because before she gave herself to anyone else, she needed to know one thing: Did Michael even remember she was alive when she wasn't with him? Did she really matter to him, outside of the stolen moments in his apartment or office?

Chapter 13

Michael

Another Sunday rolled around, and the boys were sitting outside on the lanai, sipping wine and talking. The home-cooked smell of Sunday sauce being prepared trickled in from the kitchen. Vincent leaned back in his chair and eyed Michael. "Hey, what's up with you lately? Are you not getting enough action in the bedroom?"

Michael smirked, shaking his head. "What are you talking about?"

Vincent raised a brow. "You can't hide this stuff from us, Michael. We all know you. Even Beverly sees it. You're distracted. You've lost that bounce in your step. That can only mean one thing—"

"Not enough female action," Anthony cut in, grinning.

The table erupted in laughter. Michael shook his head again, trying to maintain his mask of indifference even as a sharp, unbidden memory of Verónica's smile flashed through his mind. "You guys kill me. Just because you're all married—well, Vin, you're sort of married."

They all laughed again.

"Doesn't mean all problems come from lack of sex," Michael added, trying to brush them off.

"Yeah, it does," Anthony shot back, deadpan, before the group broke into more laughter.

With a gravity that made Michael lean in, Anthony said, "Before Angela, I never understood how a man could feel so anchored, so at peace. Just knowing the person he loves is always there. No more restless nights, no more chasing shadows. I end each day certain that when the world goes quiet, I'll be in bed with her warmth pressed against me, her breathing steady in my arms—and that, to me, is everything." Michael's smile came easily enough, but behind the expression, a sudden, heavy reflectiveness took hold. He felt the dull ache of a truth he wasn't yet ready to put into words. "I'm thrilled for you, brother," he said, the words warm yet edged with a quiet resignation. "It's just not where I'm at right now."

Then Beverly stepped out, hands on her hips. "Okay, what are my brothers talking about now? Probably money. Except Michael—he's the only one still allowed to talk about girls." She smiled knowingly. "Speaking of which, how come you never bring Olivia over for Sunday dinner? You only trot her out for weddings and funerals."

Michael's response was sharper than he intended. "Because she's not my girlfriend. We have a casual friendship, nothing more."

"Casual," Anthony muttered, chuckling. "Yeah, casual, as in—sex is over, time to go home."

The boys roared with laughter again, while Beverly rolled her eyes. "You're all terrible. I'm going back inside."

Their teasing stayed with Michael long after the laughter faded. They weren't entirely wrong. He rarely let women stay over—never blurred those lines. But lately, the image of Verónica in his bed haunted him—her hair spilling across his pillow, her warmth tucked against him through the night. He didn't understand it. Didn't want to admit it. But it was there, clawing at him.

Later that night, after dinner, Michael sat with Anthony to discuss Stratus business. They dove into Solara Edge, and its progress, and their conversation gradually drifted to something more personal. Anthony leaned forward, studying him with that sharp, big-brother stare. "All right, little brother. What's really going on? You're not yourself. Is something happening in the office I should know about? Or is this really about love?"

Michael gave a short, incredulous laugh. "Love? Me? You're out of your mind."

Anthony's expression stayed serious. "Yes. Love. I haven't seen you like this since Cathy. Remember how twisted up you were back then, before you realized she wasn't the one? You ended it, and suddenly you were yourself again. Is this the same thing? Is it Olivia? Or someone you have been keeping a secret from me?"

Michael drew in a long breath, silence stretching. He wanted to speak, but the words sat like a stone in his chest. Finally, he muttered,

"I'm not yet ready to talk about it. I don't know why. I just... can't bring it to the forefront."

Anthony's voice softened but carried weight. "Maybe you're afraid to bring it to the forefront because once you do, it becomes real. Too real. And then you can't deny it anymore."

The words hit hard, as if Anthony had pierced something Michael had worked so hard to bury. His chest tightened. He swallowed. "Maybe you're right, brother. Maybe you're right. I need to process it more. I'll let you know when I'm ready."

Anthony clapped his shoulder. "It's okay, Michael. You know I'm here for you. I just want you to find what I have with Angela. You know, she changed my life. I'm a different man because of her. I've never looked at another woman since, and for me, that says something. We made a hell of a tag team back in the day, but now..." He smiled. "Now, I'm happy to let you handle all the girls all on your own."

They both laughed quietly and walked into the kitchen, where Anthony slipped his arms around Angela from behind and kissed the back of her head. Watching them, Michael felt a sharp ache of longing gnawing at him, though he buried it deep before anyone could see.

The next day, Anthony's words refused to leave him. They gnawed at the edges of every thought, persistent and sharp. Was his brother right? Was he denying the obvious? Was he running from what had already happened inside him?

He couldn't shake the truth forming in his chest—Verónica had changed him. And no matter how hard he fought it, no matter how he tried to bury it, she was in him now.

Chapter 14

Verónica

November 1st arrived faster than Verónica could have imagined. The Four Seasons Miami was a golden blur of crystal and white roses, a display of wealth so immense it made Verónica feel as though she were stepping into another world. Stratus Meridian Group had clearly spared no expense; every shimmering detail seemed designed to remind her—and everyone else—exactly how powerful they had become.

Verónica arrived early—her heart raced beneath the satin of her gown. She had chosen a dress that clung just enough to her curves, the deep red threads catching the light with every step. A daring slit traced up her thigh, and her dark hair spilled in waves over her bare shoulders. As she stepped into the ballroom, she felt the weight of eyes on her. Whispers, glances, admiration. But none of it mattered—there was only one man she wanted to see.

She scanned the room, her pulse quickening. She spotted Ralph near the bar, already chatting with a group of colleagues. He saw her, his face lighting up, and he excused himself to meet her halfway. "Verónica," he said warmly, his gaze sweeping over her. "You look... breathtaking."

She smiled politely. "Thank you, Ralph. It's beautiful here tonight."

They made small talk, Ralph introducing her to associates, steering her around the room. She listened, nodded, played the part—but her eyes drifted constantly, searching. And then she saw him.

Michael.

He stood across the ballroom, speaking with a small circle of executives. His black tuxedo fit him as if it had been crafted on his body, crisp and sharp. He held his glass with casual ease, but the set of his jaw, the quiet authority in his stance, drew every eye in the room. Verónica felt the air leave her lungs. The noise of the crowd dulled. For a suspended moment, it was just him.

As if sensing her gaze, Michael's head lifted. His eyes found hers across the sea of people. The world tilted. Heat surged through her body, her grip tightening around her clutch. Neither of them moved; neither of them looked away. That one silent glance carried more weight than words ever could.

"Verónica?" Ralph's voice broke through the haze. She blinked, dragging her attention back, forcing a polite smile. "Yes, sorry—what were you saying?"

Ralph chuckled, seemingly unaware of the silent storm happening just inches from his face. She blinked, dragging her attention back and forcing a polite smile. "I was asking if you'd like a drink."

"Of course," she murmured.

But when Ralph left to fetch it, she dared to glance back. Michael was still watching her. This time, when their eyes met, he gave the faintest tilt of his head—an unspoken summons. Her heart hammered, her knees threatening to give way.

The night stretched on, filled with speeches, applause, and laughter.

Anthony spoke for just a few minutes, thanking the employees who work hard every day to keep Stratus Meridian Group growing. Then he introduced Michael, who took the stage. Verónica's eyes never left him. Michael spoke about the company's early days—about the risks, the long nights, and the uncertainty that marked the beginning of Stratus Meridian Group. He reminded the room how a handful of determined people had worked out of cramped offices, chasing projects bigger firms dismissed, trusting instinct and grit when experience alone wasn't enough. From those modest beginnings, he said, the company had grown into a force shaping skylines across cities, driven by people who believed in building not just structures, but communities and opportunity.

He spoke about putting everything on the line, negotiating the purchase of prime waterfront land, and spearheading the construction of Harbor Point—a towering, mixed-use skyscraper that redefined prestige, blending high-end retail, expansive commercial office space, and ultra-luxury penthouses rising above the city.

Then he also thanked the employees who had stood with them since those first uncertain years, acknowledging the loyalty, sacrifices, and countless unseen hours that made the company what it was today. Looking toward the future, he spoke with conviction about innovation, responsible development, and expanding into new markets while maintaining the values that built the firm—integrity, trust, and commitment to excellence. His voice carried an unshakeable strength, and Verónica found herself caught up in the absolute confidence he projected as he spoke. In that moment, he didn't just seem to be leading a company; he seemed to be commanding the very future itself.

Yet for Verónica, every syllable felt personal; every glance across the crowded room meant only for her. His speech lasted nearly fifteen minutes, but time dissolved into something weightless and unreal. Each time his gaze found hers, her breath caught, her legs weakened, and her pulse raced in a way that made it hard to remain steady beside the table. Ralph leaned closer to say something, but his voice faded into meaningless noise. In that moment, nothing else existed—only Michael.

After all the speeches, the band began playing, and Ralph eventually claimed his promised dance, guiding her to the floor. He held her respectfully, spinning her with practiced ease. Verónica smiled, but her heart wasn't in it. Every time she turned, she searched the room, hoping, aching.

And then, as if gravity itself had shifted, Michael appeared. He was across the room, surrounded by a small circle of people—including María, stunning as ever—yet his eyes were locked on Verónica. She felt the weight of his stare, saw his expression, and her breath stopped. It was like a hand pressed to her chest, and her heart plummeted. Had she made a mistake dancing with Ralph? Did Michael think she wanted Ralph, that she had chosen him? Couldn't he see that every beat of her heart belonged only to him? Their eyes held for a single, searing moment, and then Michael turned away sharply, as though her dancing had wounded him. The rejection cut through her like a blade.

After the dance ended, Verónica excused herself quickly and rushed to the ladies' room. She slipped into a stall, shut the door, and pressed her back against the wall, fighting the tears that threatened to spill. Her hands shook as she dabbed beneath her eyes, whispering to herself, "Don't ruin your makeup, don't let him see you break." But inside, she was unraveling. How could just one look from him undo her so completely?

By the time she returned to the table, her smile was fixed, her composure carefully stitched together. Ralph was waiting, his expression eager. "Would you like to dance again?" he asked.

Verónica forced a polite smile. "Not right now. I'd rather listen to the music and enjoy my wine."

Ralph nodded, content just to sit beside her. "Of course. I'll keep you company. You let me know when you're ready."

She thanked him with another smile, though inside she felt suffocated. Ralph's attention boxed her in, yet across the room, Michael's stare haunted her—piercing, questioning, almost accusing. Was he angry? Jealous? Or was she imagining it all, wanting so desperately for him to care that she turned every glance into hope?

Her eyes swept the room, searching for him. For one terrifying moment, she couldn't find him. Had he slipped away with María the way he had once slipped away with her at Thessaly's wedding? The thought hollowed her chest. She tried to listen to Ralph's conversation, nodding when appropriate, but her focus was gone. Every nerve in her body strained to locate Michael.

Finally, when the band paused and the dance floor cleared, she spotted him. He was seated at a table with his family and senior executives, his posture cool and unbothered. From across the empty floor, their tables faced one another. Verónica's gaze lingered, desperate for him to look up, but he didn't. Her chest tightened with dread. Maybe he really was angry. Maybe she had lost him.

Dinner passed in a blur; her appetite gone, her pulse restless. When the music started again, and the crowd surged onto the floor, she lost sight of him once more. Ralph leaned toward her. "Another dance?" he asked hopefully.

Verónica shook her head with a soft smile. "Not just yet."

Before Ralph could press, a familiar voice broke in. "Verónica, how are you?"

She looked up, and her face lit up with relief. "Beverly!" She stood and embraced her warmly. They chatted briefly—how are you, what a shame Thessaly couldn't make it, the usual pleasantries—but Verónica's heart was pounding for a different reason. She knew where Beverly could lead her. And she was right.

"I'm going to steal Verónica away for a few minutes," Beverly said sweetly, excusing herself from Ralph. "Come, I want you to meet my family."

Verónica's breath caught. Her knees went weak. Michael.

Beverly led her to the table, introducing her one by one: her husband Nick, her son Nicholas, her daughter Isabella, her brother Vincent, and Cheryl, her brother Anthony, and Angela—and then, with a knowing smile, "And of course, my brother Michael."

Michael's eyes met hers, and the world narrowed to nothing but him. "Yes, we've met," he said smoothly, his smile unreadable.

"Hello, Michael," Verónica managed, though her throat was dry. Her body screamed to collapse against him, to confess everything she felt, but she clung to composure.

Then Beverly, with a mischievous grin, sealed her fate. "Michael, Verónica isn't here with anyone. Dance with her."

Michael's eyes lingered on hers, dark with meaning, as though to say, I know what you're doing, sis. Yet he rose, extended his hand, and with a voice that made her knees tremble, asked, "Would you like to dance?"

"Yes," she whispered, her hand slipping into his. Heat exploded through her at the simple touch.

On the floor, he pulled her close, his arm firm at her waist, her hand pressed to his chest. The band played The Way You Look Tonight. Michael bent to her ear, his breath stirring her skin. "This is the perfect song for you. You look exquisite."

Her insides melted, her heart unraveling at his words. She tilted her face up to his, searching for his truth. "You know Beverly is trying to set us up," he murmured.

"You think?" She teased faintly, trying to mask the way her body was trembling.

He chuckled, low and deep. "Without a doubt." His tone shifted, becoming heavier. "I don't know if I can do this, Verónica."

She tightened her grip on him. "I don't care, Michael. Take me home tonight—even if it's only for tonight. I want to feel you again."

His breath shuddered, his control visibly fraying. But when the band shifted into a fast song, he steered her to the side, whispering urgently, "Not here. Not like this. How did you get here tonight?"

"Uber," she breathed.

"Where's your phone?"

"In my purse."

"Go back to your table. Grant will bring you his number. Call it when you're ready to leave. He will be your driver. I'll meet you at my apartment later." His gaze seared into hers. "Understand?"

Her lips curved with the barest smile. "Yes. And thank you for the dance. Or should I thank Beverly?"

Michael's grin was dangerous, promising. "I'll see you later."

The rest of the evening blurred.

She returned to Ralph, who had noticed her dancing. "I know you couldn't say no to the boss," he said with a good-natured laugh.

Verónica forced a calm smile, though heat still clung to her skin. "It was Beverly's idea. Mr. Marino was very kind."

Ralph nodded. "He's the sharpest businessman I know. A ladies' man, though—not the relationship type. Honestly, I was surprised to see him here alone."

The words stung, but Verónica kept her mask in place. If only you knew.

A little while later, Verónica caught sight of Grant standing near the bar, his tall frame cutting an imposing figure into the crowd. His eyes found hers. She lifted her chin slightly, offering him a small nod meant only as a polite greeting.

But Grant's response wasn't casual. He gave the faintest shake of his head, a silent gesture—Come here.

She let Ralph finish what he was saying before she leaned toward him and murmured, "Excuse me, I need to powder my nose."

Before he could question her, she turned, heels clicking softly against the polished floor as she made her way toward the ladies' room, stopping at the bar to see Grant. Her heart pounded, each step quickening the anticipation building inside her.

Grant didn't waste time. The moment she reached him, his large hand moved casually, smoothly, slipping a small card into hers as though he were shaking her hand hello. His lips barely moved, but his voice was firm, low enough only for her to hear. "Call me when you're ready."

The card burned against her palm, heavy with implication. She curled her fingers around it tightly, as if holding onto a secret too dangerous to expose. Her throat felt dry, her body trembling with a rush of adrenaline she couldn't tame.

Without another word, she continued on her way, pushing through the crowd until she reached the sanctuary of the ladies' room. Inside, she slipped into an empty stall and closed the door behind her, her breath coming quick, shallow.

She leaned back against the cool marble wall, pressing a hand to her chest as if she could slow the frantic rhythm of her heart. The anticipation of being with Michael later was consuming her.

By the time she returned to the table, her face betrayed nothing, though inside her veins still hummed with restless electricity.

When the night wound down, Ralph invited her to join him and others at Temple South Beach, a sleek, high-end bar in Miami. She declined gently, claiming her girlfriend was picking her up. She thanked him for his company, hiding her anticipation beneath polite words.

But when the lobby emptied and the noise of departures faded, Verónica slipped away to a quiet corner. With shaking hands, she pulled out the card and dialed.

"Grant? It's Verónica. I'm ready."

He answered immediately. "Ms. Verónica, I'll be waiting at the east door."

Moments later, she was sliding into the familiar black Range Rover, her body buzzing with anticipation. For the first time, she admitted the truth to herself: she was falling in love with Michael Marino. The thought terrified her, thrilled her, consumed her.

By the time George, the doorman, ushered her into Michael's penthouse, her heart was pounding so violently she could hear it in her ears. The lights dimmed to perfection at the touch of a button. She turned on the turntable, and Sinatra's voice filled the air—The Way You Look Tonight—the same song they had just shared. Verónica never really listened to Sinatra much, as he was well before her generation. Although Michael was only four years older than her, she remembered how he told her he loved Sixties music. He said it was a carry-down from his parents, who listened to it often. That generation had class and style, he would say, something he admired.

Verónica melted into the music, sinking into the couch, her body trembling with anticipation. She closed her eyes, remembering the heat of Michael's hand at her waist, the weight of his chest beneath her palm, the scent of his skin. Tonight, she would feel it all again.

Chapter 15

Verónica

Just as a different Sinatra song drifted into silence on the turntable, Verónica heard the smooth sound of the elevator door opening. Her breath caught. Slowly, she turned from the couch, eyes lifting just as the door swung open. Michael stepped in, filling the space with his presence. Their gazes locked—an unspoken current sparking between them, stealing her breath, stealing time itself. Her heart pounded so hard she could hear it, but her body froze, suspended between longing and fear, not knowing whether to move, speak, or run into his arms.

Michael shrugged off his jacket, tossing it carelessly onto the couch. His steps were steady and deliberate until he stood before her and extended his hand. Her fingers slipped into his, trembling under the weight of everything she felt but couldn't voice. He gently pulled her to her feet, drew her close, and his mouth claimed hers in a kiss that was searing, endless. The feel of his tongue, the taste of his lips—it was everything she had ached for in silence. She never wanted it to end.

When he finally broke the kiss, his voice was hoarse, threaded with truth. "I've missed you. God, I know I'm not the right one for you, but I've missed you."

Tears pooled in Verónica's eyes, spilling down her cheeks with a joy so sharp it almost hurt. Her voice cracked, heavy with all she had buried. "I know this is only for tonight. I know I want more than you're willing to give, but damn it, Michael—I know it's crazy, but I think I'm falling in love with you."

Shock flickered across his face. He froze, staring at her, chest rising with uneven breaths. "You can't love me," he rasped. "You shouldn't love me. We both know I'm not what you need. I don't deserve your love. You deserve someone who can give you everything you need." His hand cupped her face, thumb brushing away a tear, eyes dark and conflicted. "But I would be lying if I said I've ever felt more content, more fulfilled, than when I'm holding you like this."

Her tears deepened, mingling with the fire building inside her. Never had she felt so much at once—desire, sorrow, passion, devotion. Her entire being burned for him. With sudden, raw need, Michael swept her into his arms and carried her into the bedroom.

The bed was immaculate, crisp white sheets turned down as though prepared for them. He laid her down gently, stretching beside her, kissing her slowly at first, then deeper, until their tongues tangled in a desperate rhythm.

Her gown still clung to her body, satin against her skin, the long slit revealing flashes of her thigh. Michael's hand roamed upward, caressing her breast through the fabric, pausing, teasing, until her breath came out in shuddering waves. His fingers traveled down to the slit, sliding up the length of her leg until they found the damp heat of her thong. She gasped, hips arching instinctively toward his touch.

"Let me help you out of this gown," he whispered, his lips brushing her ear.

She gave him a trembling smile, sitting up to undo the clasp at the back. The gown loosened, slipping down her shoulders, revealing her breasts to his hungry gaze. He caught the fabric midway, unable to resist. His mouth closed over her breasts, tongue teasing, sucking, until her nipples hardened in his mouth. She moaned, the sound deep and helpless, and he shifted from one breast to the other, his hands never ceasing their worship.

Finally, he slid the gown away completely, leaving her in only her thong and heels. He kissed a trail down her legs, slow, deliberate, igniting every nerve. He took her ankle in his hand, removed her heel, and pressed his lips to the delicate arch of her foot, then sucked her perfectly manicured French-polished toes and back around. She moaned, overwhelmed, the sensation new, intimate, unbearable in its sweetness. He repeated the same reverence on her other foot, his tongue tracing up her calf, her thigh, until she trembled with anticipation.

When his hand slid her thong off, her knees parted instinctively, inviting him. Michael lowered himself between her thighs, his lips tasting her juices, his tongue circling and stroking her sweet spot with expert precision. Her body jolted, a cry escaping her throat. "Oh my God, Michael... what you do to me—please don't stop."

At her plea, his mouth moved with renewed purpose. His tongue pressed harder, faster, his thumb sliding inside her as his lips and tongue as sensation overwhelmed her. She screamed his name, muffling her cries into the pillow, her body shuddering violently. The climax tore through her, wave after wave, until she shook so hard she could barely breathe.

Michael held her, steadying her trembling body, kissing her thighs, her stomach, her breasts, before claiming her mouth again. She met him with a deep, desperate kiss, then seized his hand, the same hand that had undone her, and brought his thumb to her lips. Her mouth sucked it, and her tongue caressed it; her eyes never leaving his. "I can't believe the way you make me explode," she whispered against his skin. "So deep... so powerful. I never knew it could be this real."

Her chest still heaved, her body still quivered, but her eyes burned with need. Verónica's voice was barely a whisper. "Why do you always have your pants on when you make me feel like this?"

Michael smiled faintly, his fingers brushing against her cheek. "Two reasons," he said. "First, because I can't tell you how much joy it gives me to make it about you—about making you feel magnificent, making you feel like the most desirable woman in the world, because you are. Second..." He pressed a soft kiss to her lips, his breath warm against her skin. "If I were bare, Verónica, I wouldn't be able to control myself. You have no idea how much your body excites me."

Her lips curved into a knowing smile. "If what I feel is anything like what you feel, then yes—I know exactly."

Their eyes locked, fire rekindling between them. She leaned closer, her lips brushing his ear. "Now...it's my turn."

With slow, deliberate precision, she unbuckled his belt and released the clasp, her fingers teasing and confident. She slid down the bed, tugging his trousers off and letting them fall carelessly beside her gown. His black briefs followed, landing in the same pile, leaving Michael stretched out bare before her.

Verónica's breath caught as her gaze roamed over him. Her voice trembled with awe and desire. "Michael... you're gorgeous. Every inch of you."

He grinned, pulling her toward him for a kiss. Their lips met with hungry, unrestrained urgency, tongues tangling with raw need. When she finally broke away, her eyes smoldered with determination. "Stay right there," she whispered, pressing a finger to his chest. "It's my turn."

She trailed kisses along his neck, lingering at the curve of his collarbone, then lower over the hard lines of his chest. Her hand slid downward, fingers curling around the heat of him, and she gasped softly. "This..." she murmured, stroking him slowly, "this makes me lose my mind. It makes me ache for you."

Lowering herself, Verónica let her tongue tease the length of him, licking along his shaft, tasting his skin, before closing her lips around the tip. She took him deeper and deeper, her rhythm steady, deliberate, until she felt him twitch against her throat.

Michael's head fell back against the pillows, a groan breaking from him. "God, Verónica... you feel incredible."

She pulled back just enough to whisper, lips grazing his skin. "Do you want me to finish you with my mouth?"

His hand tangled in her hair, gently urging her up. "Not now," he growled, voice thick with need. "I want to be inside you."

He reached for the nightstand, tearing open a condom wrapper. Verónica snatched it from him, eyes gleaming. "No, let me." Slowly, teasingly, she rolled it down over his rigid length, her touch making him groan again.

She leaned back, parting her thighs, her voice husky. "Now, Michael. I need you."

He positioned himself above her; the head of his manhood nudging against her wet lower lips. Her hands gripped his hips as she urged him closer. "Please... put it inside me."

With one deep, steady thrust, he slid into her. Both gasped at the same moment; the connection was overwhelming. He began moving, slowly at first, then harder, faster, until the sound of her cries filled the room.

"Deeper, Michael... deeper!" she moaned, arching against him.

He grasped her butt, lifting her to meet his thrusts, burying himself inside her until he struck that spot that unraveled her completely. She screamed, her cries shattering beneath him as her body convulsed in release.

Michael didn't stop. He drove into her, his thrusts turning urgent and uncontrolled, a raw groan tearing from his throat as she felt him pulsing inside her as he released, his body collapsing against hers.

For a long, breathless moment, neither moved. Their hearts pounded in sync, bodies tangled, lips finding each other again in a deep, consuming kiss.

When he finally withdrew, he rolled to his side, pulling her against him. His arms wrapped tight around her, refusing to let go.

"I know I shouldn't, but I love you, Michael," Verónica whispered, her voice breaking as tears welled in her eyes. "I love you."

He buried his face in her hair, holding her as if he never wanted to let go. His words came rough, pained. "Verónica... please don't. You deserve better than me. So much better."

Her hand pressed to his chest, feeling the frantic beat of his heart. "I don't care. I don't want better. I don't want anyone else. If this is all I can have with you, the only way I can see you, then I'll take it. No one... no one makes me feel the way you do."

Chapter 16
Michael

They had fallen asleep tangled in each other's arms, their bodies refusing to let go even in sleep. When the sunlight spilled across the room, Michael stirred, blinking against the brightness. For the briefest moment, he thought he was dreaming. Verónica was still wrapped around him, her face pressed to his chest, her breath soft and steady.

He froze, startled by the realization. That has never happened before. Not even years ago, when he clung to the illusion that his relationship with Cathy was real and lasting. He had never allowed himself to drift into sleep holding someone like this, never woken to find a woman still clinging to him as though she belonged there. It unsettled him—and yet, something about it made his chest tighten in ways he couldn't understand.

Her lashes fluttered open, and her eyes, still hazy with sleep, met his. A slow, delicate smile spread across her lips. Michael bent and kissed her softly, unable to stop himself.

"What time is it?" she whispered.

He reached for his phone, glanced at the screen, and gave a short laugh. "Almost ten. I can't believe it."

Verónica's eyes widened. "Ten? I'm usually at Mass by now."

Michael smirked. "I don't think you're making it this morning."

"Do you go every week?" he asked.

"Yes," she whispered, her expression tender. "I've gone for as long as I can remember. My mom always came with me before she passed away about five years ago. Since then, I usually go alone." Her voice carried a quiet ache.

Michael hesitated. "What about your ex?"

Her jaw tightened. "No. He thought church was for losers. Even when we married, he refused to take our vows in a church. My mom warned me I was making a mistake. I should have listened."

Michael gave a faint, sad smile. "Isn't that always the truth? Moms know best."

She studied him for a moment. "Do you ever go?"

He chuckled dryly. "I'm not sure the walls wouldn't shake if I walked in. I haven't been to church since I was a kid. My mother went faithfully, but... once we got older, none of us boys followed. Maybe after my mother died, there was no one left to encourage us to go. Seeing her go through cancer was hard for all of us. I think it changed each of us in different ways, since Beverly still goes to church. She always tells me I need to go—it would be good for me. But I never feel the urge."

Before she could respond, he tugged her close again. "Come here."

Their lips met, but Verónica pulled back with a laugh. "Michael, morning breath."

Michael grinned, unfazed. "I don't care. And I'm not letting you out of this bed."

He felt Verónica's resistance melt; he felt the warmth and need surging through her. She wrapped her arms around his neck, kissing him with a passion that silenced every other thought but the rush of desire. His leg found her, claiming the warmth between her legs, while his fingers teased her breasts until her nipples hardened, drawing soft moans that filled the room. His mouth continued to tease her nipples, coaxing sounds of pleasure from her lips.

Her body trembled with hunger as he moved down her stomach, lips and tongue tracing every inch. His hands gently coaxed her thighs apart, and the first brush of his tongue against her sweet spot made her cry out. She clutched the sheets, her body arching in rhythm to his movements. Her moans grew louder, each one breaking more of her control. Michael slipped a hand under her butt, lifting her slightly closer to him, while his tongue worked relentlessly. As he slid his thumb inside her, the dam broke. She screamed as he continued to please her, her body exploding in wave after wave of release, rocking her world again and again.

He stayed with her, coaxing her through it. When he felt her body relax, he lifted his face from between her trembling thighs, slick with her ecstasy. His eyes locked on hers as he licked his finger slowly. "You taste incredible," he murmured.

Verónica pulled him up into a desperate, soul-deep kiss. "Oh, Michael, I can't believe what you do to me. I need you inside me," she whispered, "Now."

Michael reached for a condom, sliding it over his hard, erect length as her breath came in sharp, impatient gasps. She lay back, open and wanting, and when he entered her, the cry that escaped her throat was part pain, part bliss. "Yes," she moaned, clutching him tighter, "you feel so amazing."

Their bodies moved in a desperate rhythm, clashing and building together. She begged for more, pulling him deeper, her nails grazing his back as he drove them higher and higher. Her moans grew louder and louder, echoing through the room. When release shattered her once more, it pulled him along. He buried his face in her neck, his climax tearing through him, his groan muffled against her skin.

Breathless and still slick with sweat, they clung to each other. Michael kissed Verónica's damp forehead, and she looked up at him, her eyes shining, lips trembling. "I know you don't want me to, but I love you, Michael."

His chest tightened. The words reverberated in his mind, dangerously close to the ones he longed to say back. Fear, however, silenced him, leaving only the weight of unsaid truths.

They lay together in quiet until the clock reminded him of reality. "I hate to say this, but I have to get ready to see my dad."

She smiled weakly. "I should get some work done before Ralph complains the contracts aren't done."

Michael's tone sharpened. "If he complains to you, you tell me."

Her lips curved. "He'll be fine."

They rose and showered, the intimacy between them lingering even as they prepared to dress. When Verónica emerged from the bathroom wrapped in only a towel, she frowned. "Michael, I can't believe I'm in this position again. I only have my gown to wear home."

He smirked. "Wait here."

Michael disappeared into another room and returned carrying two enormous shopping bags from Violet & Grace, an upscale boutique in South Beach. He handed them to her. "Take your pick," he said.

Verónica peered inside, stunned to see an assortment of clothes. Sweatpants, shorts, bras, thongs, sneakers, flats, and a variety of tops filled the bags. Sizes varied, giving her options.

"What is this?" she whispered.

"Once I saw your name on the guest list for the gala, I knew there was a chance we'd wind up here. I figured you'd face the same problem again," he explained. "So I sent someone to pick up a few things for you. I wasn't sure of your exact size, so... I told her to give you options."

Her eyes softened, her heart swelling. "This is the most thoughtful thing anyone's ever done for me. See why I love you?" She arched an eyebrow. "Who picked these out? Please don't say María."

Michael chuckled, shaking his head. "No, it wasn't María."

He tilted his head, confusion flickering in his eyes. "Why her, though?"

Verónica hesitated, chewing her bottom lip, before asking what had been quietly gnawing at her. "It's none of my business, and I have no right to ask, but... can I ask you something?"

Michael leaned against the couch, arms relaxed, admiring her. "Sure."

Her chest rose with a quick breath. "Have you and María ever been... a thing? Has she ever visited you here?"

Michael blinked, clearly surprised, then gave a low laugh. "No—to both questions. But why would you think that?"

Verónica's voice dropped, almost a whisper, but sharp with honesty. "Because she treats me like the enemy. Either she's been with you, or she wants to be—and somehow she seems to think I'm the threat that stands in her way."

Michael laughed again, but this time it carried a dangerous amusement rather than dismissal. He stepped closer, his presence consuming the space between them, and slipped his arms around her waist. "I know exactly what María wants. But I don't mix business and pleasure. Company rule."

Verónica tilted her chin, eyes locked on his, fierce and unyielding. "Yet here you are," she whispered, her voice trembling with both defiance and desire.

Michael's smile darkened. "You're right," he murmured. "I'm breaking that rule with you."

This time, when his lips brushed hers, Verónica didn't let him lead. She tightened her grip on his shirt, pulling him down to her, pressing her mouth harder to his, claiming the kiss for herself. The softness of his kiss was met with her hunger, her insistence, her need to make him understand she was no passing distraction.

She took the shopping bags into the bathroom and tried on the clothes, emerging like a model from a dressing room. She chose soft red shorts, white Tory Burch sneakers, and a white, long, soft T-shirt tied at the side. Michael's eyes raked over her. "Perfect. You look incredible."

Verónica laughed, shaking her head. "Maybe I should meet this woman who shopped for me. She has good taste."

Michael smiled; his voice held a tinge of regret. "I'm sorry, I can't stay for lunch."

Verónica leaned in before he could pull away. "Then I'll take a rain check," she replied quickly, refusing to let him escape without sensing her presence.

His mouth curved into a small smile, but tension lingered in his eyes. "Grant is waiting downstairs for you. He'll take you wherever you want to go."

Michael watched her tilt her head, his gaze tracking the subtle shift in her expression. He could almost see the gears turning behind those dark eyes. For a moment, the poised, professional woman he'd first met seemed to resurface—the one who would simply offer a polite thank you, gather her pride, and walk out of his apartment without looking back.

But as the silence stretched, that mask of professionalism began to crack. Michael felt the air between them thicken with a renewed, wordless hunger. She didn't look like a woman ready to fade into the background of his life; there was a flicker of defiance in her gaze, a silent promise that she wouldn't be so easily dismissed. He could still smell the faint, intoxicating scent of her perfume, and he had the distinct impression that even if she left now, she intended to leave a permanent mark on his conscience.

A sudden, playful light kindled in her eyes, catching him off guard. She glanced toward her discarded gown and heels, then turned back to him. The heavy tension of the moment broke as a teasing tone slipped into her voice.

"If I'm truly leaving," she said, her tone a deliberate, sultry challenge, "can I at least borrow one of the shopping bags to carry my gown and heels home?"

Michael felt a reluctant smile tug at the corner of his mouth. He knew she was testing him, poking at his resolve to see if it would crumble again. She looked entirely too comfortable in his space, and despite his better judgment, he found himself wanting to give her whatever she asked for just to keep her there a few minutes longer.

"Take both shopping bags—and whatever is in them. I bought them for you," he said firmly. "What doesn't fit, or what you don't like, bring back and exchange it for what works."

Michael watched her closely, tracking the way her gaze skipped over the designer logos. She looked overwhelmed, her breath hitching as she stared at the sheer volume of luxury he'd laid at her feet. There was a warring tension in her posture, as if she were caught between the desire to sink into the gifts and the instinct to run from the weight of such an extravagant gesture.

"I can't do that," she protested softly, her voice barely a whisper. "It's bad enough you bought me all these expensive clothes, Michael. I could never afford to shop in a place like that."

Michael didn't waver. He leaned against the edge of his bed, enjoying the flush that climbed her neck. He knew exactly what he was doing—he was marking her, ensuring his presence followed her home in the form of every seam and button.

"Take them home," he said, his tone casual but firm. "Exchange what doesn't fit. If you don't, they'll just sit here taking up space. Or," he added, a sudden, wicked thought occurring to him, "maybe I'll just give them away to someone else in the office. Maybe María would like them."

He watched for the reaction, and he wasn't disappointed. The moment the name left his lips, Verónica's entire demeanor shifted. Her shoulders stiffened, and a sharp, unmistakable flash of possessiveness flared in her eyes. It was a beautiful sight—the predatory spark of a woman who had no intention of letting another soul touch what belonged to her.

She narrowed her eyes at him, the hesitation vanishing in an instant, replaced by a slow, dangerous smile that tugged at the corner of her lips.

"In that case," she said, her voice dropping into a tone of playful defiance as she reached for the bags, "give me the shopping bags."

Michael felt a surge of satisfaction. He'd poked the lioness, and she'd come out to play. As she gripped the handles, he realized he didn't just want her wearing his clothes—he wanted her exactly like this, fierce and claiming him just as clearly as he was claiming her.

Their laughter filled the air, but beneath it was an unspoken tension neither could release. He walked her to the elevator door, and when he leaned in to kiss her, it wasn't rushed—it was gentle, lingering, enough to leave her breathless. His lips barely brushed hers before he whispered, "You're making me think, Verónica. That's very dangerous for me."

Michael watched her, looking for any sign of the nerves that had gripped her only moments ago. She didn't let so much as a tremor show. Instead, she tilted her chin, her lips curving into a slow, knowing smile that hit him like a physical blow. It was a look of pure, dangerous challenge—as if she were daring him to try to handle the fire she'd just started.

"Good," she breathed. The word was a soft, vibrating hum that lingered in the air long after she turned away.

He didn't move, his gaze locked on her as she walked toward the elevator. Every step she took was measured; the fluid sway of her hips radiating a sudden, lethal confidence. She didn't look back, and Michael realized she didn't have to; she knew exactly what she was doing to him. As the elevator closed, the silence of the apartment felt suddenly heavy, charged with the lingering electricity of her presence and a sharp, undeniable hunger that left him wanting more.

Once she was gone, Michael put on music as he dressed for his father's house. But no matter how loud the song, he couldn't drown the storm inside him. What has she done to me? What box has she opened? He asked himself.

He had wanted to tell her he loved her, wanted to let the words slip free, but he couldn't. He wouldn't. Love was the one thing he refused himself. And yet, he did not know how to forget her now.

Chapter 17

Verónica

After leaving Michael's apartment, Verónica stepped through the lobby doors to find Grant waiting by the car. He straightened when he saw her, opening the door with his usual calm professionalism.

"Hello," she greeted softly, offering a smile.

"So nice to see you again, Ms. Verónica," he replied warmly.

She slid into the back seat, sinking into the leather and resting her head against it. Her heart was still racing, her body still humming from the hours spent in Michael's arms. She replayed every detail in her mind—how he touched her, how he looked at her, how he made her feel as though she were the only woman in the world. The memory wrapped around her like a warm, intimate caress, reminding her why she loved him, why she couldn't let go no matter how hard she tried.

The gesture with the clothes—so unexpected, so thoughtful—had pierced straight through her defenses. It felt as though he saw her, knew her in a way no one else ever had. And yet, doubts slipped in like unwelcome shadows. He hadn't asked to see her tomorrow or suggested making plans for the week. He hadn't said the words she longed for when she whispered she loved him. Instead, he told her not to love him. He hadn't even asked for her number, as if sweet texts between them were impossible luxuries. So many didn'ts... so many ways he kept her at arm's length.

But she told herself this was Michael. This was who he was. And if accepting him meant taking what he offered without asking for more, then she would do it. She would rather have him in pieces than not have him at all.

Her phone chimed with a text, startling her. For a heartbeat, her heart leapt—please, let it be him. Please let him say he missed her already, that he couldn't wait to see her again, that she should come back. But it wasn't Michael. It was Susan.

> Hey, babe, are you home? Free later? I'll be in the area.

Verónica sighed, torn between disappointment and relief. She missed Susan—her energy, her laughter, the way she could pull her out of her own head. And maybe it would be good to have a distraction tonight. She typed back quickly,

> I'll be home tonight. Come over, and we can catch up.

> See you at 7

When Susan arrived, they hugged tightly before settling onto the couch. Verónica opened the wine Susan had brought, grateful for the comfort of her friend's presence.

"Tell me about Italy," Verónica said, eager to steer the conversation away from her own aching heart.

"Italy was wonderful. The shoot was perfect, and I met this gorgeous Italian businessman who wined and dined me, and fucked my brains out for a week," Susan winked.

"You're amazing," Verónica laughed, shaking her head.

Susan leaned closer, lowering her voice with mock secrecy. "Sex with an Italian? Very exciting. Very romantic in the bedroom, if you know what I mean."

They both laughed, but inside, Verónica's chest tightened as she thought—I know exactly what you mean.

"So, Susan prodded," tell me about your love life. How are things with Ralph? Did you do him yet?

"Stop, Susan," Verónica said with a playful swat. "No, I didn't do Ralph. He's a client."

Susan arched an eyebrow. "Don't you think he wants to do you?"

Verónica shook her head again, pouring them both more wine.

"Honey," Susan pressed, "you need to get some action in the bed-room, or you'll never forget about Gregory. Who, if I remember correctly, doesn't know the first thing about pleasing a woman."

"Forget who?" Verónica teased, her tone light, and they both dissolved into laughter.

"You're right about one thing," she admitted between chuckles. "Gregory doesn't have a clue about how to please a woman in the bedroom." Their laughter echoed again, but behind Verónica's smile, her mind was already drifting.

As Susan went on about her latest escapade, Verónica felt herself slipping away into memory. Michael. His name throbbed in her chest like a secret heartbeat. She wanted to tell Susan everything—the way he kissed her, how his touch ignited every corner of her body, how he gave her pleasures she hadn't even known she was capable of feeling. How he set her free and chained her heart in the same breath. But she couldn't. She dared not. Susan's tongue was too loose, her circle too wide. A secret like Michael wouldn't survive her friend's gossip. If Thessaly found out, if Beverly heard, the whispers might reach him, and everything could unravel.

So instead, she smiled and nodded, clutching her secret close like a bruise she pressed but wouldn't show. It ached in silence, a sweet torment she endured alone.

They ordered pizza, Sicilian style, Susan's choice. They poured more cheap red wine, Malbec from Australia, trading stories the way only old friends could. Susan's adventures spilled out like scenes from a movie—wild, fearless, reckless in ways Verónica had never dared to be. She listened with a mixture of envy and admiration. Susan was bold, unashamed, untethered by consequences. Maybe Susan would be perfect for Michael, she thought bitterly—the idea stabbing her chest. Then, with a sudden surge of protectiveness, another thought seared through her—if Susan ever tried, I would scratch her eyes out.

When Susan finally left, she kissed her on the cheek and said with a grin, "Don't forget, honey—you need to find some action."

Verónica smiled, waved her off, and closed the door. But the moment she was alone again, the ache surged back, heavier than before.

She poured another glass of wine and curled onto the couch, the rim of the glass trembling in her fingers. The silence pressed in around her, thick and merciless, leaving nothing but her thoughts—and every single one circling back to Michael.

His hands. His lips. The low, commanding timbre of his voice. She could still feel the weight of his body against hers, the way his touch had unraveled her until she was nothing but need. Her heart ached as the questions spilled in, one after another. Would he ever want more than these stolen, magnificent, dangerous moments? Would she ever be more to him than a secret he kept locked away behind his perfect control?

Her mind replayed the look in his eyes when she mentioned she didn't want Ralph to give her a hard time if the contracts were late—how his jaw had tightened, how a flash of protectiveness had cut through his usual polished composure. If he didn't care, why would it matter to him? Why couldn't he just face what was between them instead of pushing her away, instead of pretending she didn't matter?

She pressed the glass to her lips, but the wine no longer dulled the ache in her chest. The longing twisted deeper, burning. She wanted him—not tomorrow, not when it was convenient, but now. She wanted to take control, to make him see she wasn't fragile, wasn't a distraction, wasn't just another woman he could cast aside. She wanted to show him that what they shared was real, undeniable, and worth every risk.

The questions followed her like a chill that wouldn't lift. She forced herself to pick up the contracts, to drown in the black-and-white language until her vision blurred. She worked until her head grew heavy, until exhaustion wrapped around her shoulders. But even as sleep claimed her, it was Michael's face that lingered in her mind—his mouth against hers, his voice in her ear. And in her dreams, she didn't wait for him to claim her. In her dreams, she claimed him.

Chapter 18
Michael

Michael walked out of his apartment, still wrapped in the fading trace of Verónica's perfume. It clung to his shirt, to his skin, as though he had a permanent stain. Sliding into his red Ferrari, he put the top down, turned on some music, and cruised down Collins Avenue toward his father's house. The Miami sun burned bright, and the ocean breeze rushed over him. But none of it mattered—his thoughts belonged only to her. Her scent, her touch, the fire in her eyes. He was consumed, and there was no escaping it.

Pulling up behind the family cars already lined up out front—a lineup of cars that screamed Marino success. Of course, he was the last to arrive. He paused for a moment, staring at the house, and the weight of something he hadn't felt in years pressed down on him. Why was he always the only one walking into this house alone? His sister, Beverly, had already built her own bustling world, anchored by a husband and two children who carried the weight of family history. Her son, Nicholas, bore his father's name, while Isabella had been named after their mother—who, in Michael's memory, had once filled these rooms with life. Anthony, his partner in their club days, had long since traded the nightlife for Angela, the love of his life. Vincent had Cheryl steady at his side, no matter the hours or secrets his work demanded.

Once, Michael reveled in being the unattached one, the wild card. He had liked the freedom, the endless possibilities, the thrill of never being tied down. Change women like changing suits—that had been his motto. But walking in now, he felt only the hollowness of it. Empty. Alone. What the hell had happened to him?

The door swung open. Beverly stood there, grinning. "Finally, my baby brother shows up. Rough night?" She chuckled.

Michael smirked, brushing past her with a kiss on the cheek. "Overslept."

Anthony shoved a glass of wine into his hand. "One of these days, Michael, you're going to find someone who makes you want to settle down."

Michael only nodded, lips curving into a polite smile. But inside, his chest tightened. He had already found her—he was just too damn scared to admit it.

Anthony clapped his hands and called for everyone's attention. "Angela and I have some news," he said, slipping his arm around her waist. His voice warmed as he added, "There's going to be another Marino in the family."

A chorus of congratulations filled the room. Beverly whooped, "That's why you're not drinking with me, Angela!" Everyone laughed. Anthony's face glowed with pride; every word carried it. Michael hugged his brother, happy for him—truly happy—but as the celebration swirled around him, something sharp and numbing gnawed at his core. Why did joy for them feel like emptiness for him? Why did his mind instantly leap to Verónica? What if she were pregnant? The thought cut him in half—dangerous, impossible. He shook it off. He was a businessman, not a dreamer.

His phone buzzed. For one reckless heartbeat, his pulse surged—could it be her?—but he stopped himself cold. He hadn't even given her his number. How absurd that thoughts of her carrying his child when they hadn't even exchanged that simplest piece of communication could haunt him.

It was Olivia. Of course. He rolled his eyes at the text.

> Hey, I assume you're at your dad's. Want to swing by later?

He waited twenty minutes before replying, polite but detached.

> Thanks for the offer, but I'm beat. Big week ahead with Solara Edge.

She wrote back quickly,

Okay, talk soon.

But Michael knew he was lying to them both. He had no desire to see her again. His heart—and his body—already belonged to someone else.

Driving home, the emptiness pressed harder. The city lights blurred past him, neon and noise, but he barely noticed. By the time he stepped into his apartment, he felt wrung out. He poured himself a short single malt, set Sinatra spinning on the turntable, and dropped onto the couch. The leather felt cold against his back, his apartment colder still.

"This is the life," he muttered. "The penthouse, the cars, the money. Women at my feet. And I'm sitting here like a hollow man, because she isn't here."

Anthony's joy with Angela gnawed at him. Maybe he was seeing the truth for the first time—that life wasn't just about money, or deals, or conquests. Maybe it was about waking up next to someone who made the world feel right. He rubbed his face. "God, I wish Mom were here. She'd know what to say to me." Maybe Beverly too—but how could he confess Verónica to her? The one woman he couldn't stop thinking about was the one woman he shouldn't want.

He let the scotch burn down his throat and told himself to sleep it off.

The next morning, as always, discipline took over. Gym at 6 a.m., desk by 7:30. Meetings stacked back to back. He buried himself in work, but Anthony's words from the night before stuck like burrs he couldn't shake. When Anthony himself wandered into his office at dawn, Michael raised a brow.

"What the hell are you doing here so early?"

Anthony laughed. "Couldn't sleep. I'm too wound up about the baby. I woke up at five, couldn't wait to touch Angela, to feel her next to me. We even made love before breakfast. I didn't think it was possible to feel closer to her, but I do." His grin softened. "Remember when I thought the clubs, the women, the freedom was everything? I didn't have a clue, Michael. Not a damn clue."

Michael said nothing. He didn't need to. He just listened, Anthony's joy settling heavily on his chest.

At eleven sharp, Sara stepped into his office. "The managers are waiting for you in the conference room."

Michael glanced up from his desk, forced his features into a calm expression, and nodded. "I'll be right there." He slipped on his jacket, every motion precise, controlled, as if he were trying to armor himself in routine.

The conference room was already full. Project managers and their assistants sat waiting, notebooks and laptops open, expectant eyes on him. He moved to the head of the table, aware of the room following his every move. "Alright," he said, his voice steady, even. "Let's start from the left and go around."

One by one, they reported on schedule, ahead of schedule, slightly over budget—nothing he hadn't heard a hundred times before. But his focus was fractured, his thoughts not fully tethered to the updates.

Javier spoke next. "I'll be covering Ralph's projects today."

Michael's eyes flicked sharply toward him. "Where's Ralph?"

Javier cleared his throat and straightened his papers. "He had a lunch appointment with Ms. Liora."

The name struck him like a jolt to the heart. For a moment, everything inside him tightened—his pulse, his breath, the muscles across his shoulders. Verónica. Ralph was with Verónica.

Michael forced his expression to remain neutral and his voice to remain cool. "Proceed."

But beneath the mask, his insides were in chaos. Ralph. Having lunch with her. Alone. The thought twisted inside him, hot and sharp, a mix of jealousy and something far more dangerous. He clasped his hands in front of him on the table, listening as Javier continued with updates he could barely register.

Another manager spoke, her words a blur, until finally the last report was given.

"Thank you," Michael said, his voice clipped, efficient. "I appreciate the updates." He pushed back his chair and walked out of the room, the pressure in his chest nearly suffocating him.

Alone, he sat at his desk, fists tightening. The thought of Ralph leaning toward her, smiling at her, touching her—a wave of anger roared through him. He wanted to put his fist through the wall. Jealousy. Raw, vicious jealousy. A feeling he'd never allowed himself before.

He grabbed his phone and called Grant. "Give me the number Verónica called you from the night of the gala."

Grant, surprised, hesitated but obeyed. Michael saved it, staring at her name on the screen. He could call her. He could open that door wide and never close it again. But instead, he slammed the phone down.

He picked up his desk phone and called Ralph's secretary. Abruptly, he said, "Tell Ralph I want him in my office the minute he's back."

Not long after, Ralph phoned. "Michael, I heard you were looking for me. Is there a problem?"

Michael's voice was ice. "Where are you, Ralph?"

"I'm at Osteria del Mar with Verónica, I mean Ms. Liora."

"Verónica," Michael snapped. "Getting pretty friendly, aren't you?"

Ralph stammered. "No, sir, just business. Contracts, timelines—"

"You missed a manager's meeting for it." Michael's tone sharpened. "If you can't make those meetings, maybe Javier should have your job."

"No, Michael—it won't happen again."

"Enjoy your lunch." Michael ended the call, jaw tight.

When Ralph finally appeared in his doorway half an hour later, nervous and apologetic, Michael didn't soften. He leaned forward, voice low and dangerous. "You know the rules. Business and pleasure don't mix. Not in my company. You cross that line, you're finished. Am I clear?"

"Yes, Michael."

Ralph left quickly.

Alone again, Michael leaned back in his chair. Hypocrite. That's what he had become. He wanted to burn Ralph to the ground for even breathing the same air as her, while he himself couldn't stop imagining her in his bed again. He closed his eyes. What the hell was he supposed to do now? Stop seeing Verónica completely? Stop caring about her. He could try, but he knew his heart would fight him every step of the way.

Chapter 19

Verónica

Verónica tried to bury herself in her work, telling herself she could put Michael on the back burner. Her desk was stacked with the last batch of Solara Edge contracts, and she attacked them with a determination that almost bordered on obsession. If she couldn't have him, then she would pour her heart into the one thing she could control—her career.

Peter passed her office, leaning in with an approving smile. "Verónica, I just want to tell you—you're doing a magnificent job. This Stratus Meridian Group deal you brought in is going to make the year for Delgado, Mercer & Klein LLP. Honestly, it could make your career. You might even be in line for partner one day."

She smiled politely, thanked him, but her chest ached with bittersweet truth. She knew her hard work mattered—but the only reason she had this chance was Michael. Michael had opened the door to Stratus Meridian Group. Michael had opened her heart. He was the reason she now understood what true love could feel like, and why it hurt so much to be without it.

Later, as she poured herself coffee in the break room, a man walked in with a confident smile. "Hi, I'm Walter Brennan. I don't think we've met."

Verónica turned, offering a polite smile as she shook his hand. "Nice to meet you." He was well-dressed and decent-looking, and he clearly thought she should be impressed by him.

"I practice tax law," he said, studying her. "I hear you're quickly becoming a commercial contracts expert."

"I wouldn't go that far," she replied coolly. "But I enjoy it." She could sense the probing nature of his attention and excused herself quickly, coffee in hand.

Back in her office, Caroline, a girl in the secretarial pool Verónica had become friendly with, slipped in and shut the door behind her. "I noticed you talking with Walter in the break room. Just so you know," she whispered, "Walter's been asking about you. I think he's got the hots for you. Be careful—I don't trust him."

Verónica raised a brow. "Funny. I just got that feeling in the break room."

Caroline leaned in. "He's a junior partner, but he throws his weight around. His brother runs with a rough Miami crowd and seems to be pretty well off, and there are rumors about Walter and some secretaries. Just—watch yourself."

"Thanks, Caroline. I appreciate the warning."

When Caroline left, Verónica sat back with a sigh. Another Gregory, she thought. Another man who thought the office was his playground. Walter might have been a playboy, but he didn't fool her. Michael might have had plenty of women, but as far as she knew, he didn't mix business with pleasure—well, not until her.

The weeks stretched on without a word from Michael—her smile faded. Silence was unbearable. She missed him desperately—his touch, his kiss, the way he made her body come alive. She wanted him. Needed him. And yet, he was nowhere.

Even Ralph seemed different. Once warm and chatty, now he was all business. Lunch invitations never came again. Something about him felt guarded.

Finally, she couldn't take it anymore. On a call with Ralph to arrange a contract meeting, she casually suggested, "Instead of meeting at my office, why don't we have lunch at the new place down the street? My treat."

There was a pause, then his voice tightened. "No...let's just meet in your office."

Confusion lingered until the following week, when Ralph finally came in. They finished their contract review, and before he left, Verónica asked softly, "Ralph...is everything okay? Did I offend you?"

He hesitated, then met her eyes with something vulnerable, almost sad. "Verónica, you're the most beautiful woman I know. You're smart, classy, sexy. I'd love to have lunch or dinner with you, but if I did...I'd lose my job."

Her brows knit. "Why?"

He exhaled heavily. "I probably shouldn't tell you this, because if you repeat it, I'll be gone. The day we had lunch, when I left abruptly, my secretary called, remember? She told me Michael was furious, looking for me. I hung up and called him right away, explaining why I missed the managers' meeting, where I was, and who I was with. I thought that would suffice." Ralph gave a small, nervous laugh. "But it didn't. In fact, I think it made things worse. I thought he was going to strangle me on the phone. After I left you in the restaurant, I went straight to his office, and he told me flat out: if I so much as thought about having a personal relationship with you, I'd be gone. Javier would take over. No questions asked."

Her breath caught, pulse racing.

Ralph continued, almost apologetically. "Michael is a great boss, and I know every girl goes crazy over him. He walks into the office, and all the women drool. But in all the years I've worked for him, not once did he touch a girl from the office or a client. And trust me—his chances were endless." Ralph gave a half-smile and shook his head. "So, I accepted what he said about you. Having lunch with you is not a good idea right now. But if I ever thought I had a real chance with you, I'd think about quitting my job."

Her heart thudded. "Oh, Ralph... that's so sweet. But no. I'd never want you to lose your job. And if I'm honest... I'm already involved with someone. My heart is taken."

He nodded with a soft smile. "He's a lucky guy, whoever he is. Friends, then?"

She smiled back. "Friends."

That night, as Verónica drove home, her heart soared higher than it had in weeks. She felt light, almost weightless, as if her body couldn't contain the joy rushing through her. Michael hadn't forgotten her. He cared—he had to care. He had been jealous—jealous of Ralph, jealous of the possibility of her giving herself to another man. The realization made her chest ache with an intoxicating mixture of relief and excitement. He had wanted her badly enough to let that mask of control slip, even for a moment.

She pressed her hand against her heart, smiling into the darkness of her car. It was as if invisible arms wrapped around her, shielding her, claiming her. Michael may not have said the words aloud, but to her, his jealousy screamed them. She was his—she felt it in her bones.

By the time she reached home, she could hardly breathe. She felt protected in a way she hadn't felt in years, cherished even without a public declaration. He was fighting his demons—she was certain of it. She would give him the time he needed—time to face himself, to fight whatever ghosts haunted him. But deep down, Verónica's conviction only hardened. She believed with every fiber of her being that she was his destiny, just as much as he was hers.

Chapter 20

Michael

The Monday after Thanksgiving arrived with none of the calm that usually followed a holiday weekend. Michael sat behind his desk, already buried beneath the chaos waiting for him. Stacks of folders crowded every corner—bid comparisons from supervisors spread open across his desk, pages marked with handwritten notes and highlighted numbers demanding decisions. Half-finished contracts lay beside cold coffee, while his computer screen flashed with unanswered emails and calendar alerts stacked back-to-back for the coming weeks.

Reports from the marketing department on Solara Edge waited in thick binders at his elbow, campaign budgets flagged for approval, timelines circled in red, and presentation drafts clipped together for revisions he hadn't yet found time to review. Every few minutes, his phone buzzed with another message—project updates, financing questions, permit approvals—each reminder that construction never paused simply because he had taken a holiday weekend.

A soft knock barely registered before Sara stepped inside, expertly navigating the paper-strewn desk as she carried in the morning mail. She always filtered it first, sparing him the junk and delivering only what truly required his attention. As she set a small, carefully curated stack before him, she paused, holding one envelope aloft with a knowing grin.

"I know you hate these things," she said. "But you've been invited to the Delgado, Mercer & Klein Christmas party. December 5th. Unfortunately, this invitation somehow got lost in the mailroom. It's this Friday night."

Michael's pulse spiked. Just hearing the firm's name made Verónica flash in his mind like lightning.

"I assume I should RSVP with regrets?" Sara asked.

He shook his head slowly, staring at the envelope. "No. Let me... think about it."

Sara looked surprised. Michael rarely went to vendor parties—he always declined or sent someone else. But now, his chest ached as the thought formed: Could this be his chance to see her again? It had been weeks, but it felt like a lifetime. He missed her. God, he missed her.

Maybe the Christmas party would be the perfect excuse, the perfect moment to test what still burned between them. But then reality slapped him—this was her company party. She couldn't just vanish into a dark corner with him like before. Still, the thought of her in an evening gown, laughing, her eyes seeking him out across a crowded room—it consumed him.

For once, Michael admitted it to himself. He wasn't on top of his game. Not since the night Verónica walked into Thessaly's wedding had he truly been himself. He needed clarity, perspective—something he couldn't find alone. His brothers had always been his sounding board, but this—this was different. This was deeper. For this, he needed Beverly.

He picked up the phone and dialed.

"Wow," Beverly answered with her usual warmth. "A call from my baby brother during work hours. Did a building fall down?"

Michael laughed softly. "Funny. Hey sis—can you do dinner tonight? I need to talk."

Her voice instantly sharpened with concern. "Michael, is everything okay?"

"Yeah," he assured her. "Nothing's wrong. I just... need to pick your brain."

There was a pause, then she said gently, "I had plans, but I'll call Nick. He'll understand." She chuckled. "Though he'll probably assume a skyscraper collapsed."

They both laughed, but Michael's laugh faded into something heavier.

Ten minutes later, Beverly texted:

> 5 p.m. Where?

Michael typed back immediately:

> MILA. Fancy place for my fancy sister. Grant will pick you up at your office.

At 5:15, they were seated at a quiet, tucked-away table, champagne chilling between them. Michael had ensured privacy. If he was going to open his heart, it couldn't be where the world could hear.

After the first sip, Beverly arched an eyebrow. "So... when are you going to tell me what's going on?"

Michael smirked faintly, but his eyes betrayed him. "Bev, this is hard. I love you, but this is... different. Honestly, I wish Mom were still here. She'd know the answer. You were always there when we lost her, and right now—I need you to step in for her."

Her expression softened, and she waited, watching him carefully.

"You know, the last time I tried to be serious with someone was Cathy," he said. "She was beautiful, fun, the sex was great... but it wasn't love. Not the kind that goes deeper than the skin. When I broke it off, I swore I was done with relationships. Safer that way. But now..." He exhaled, rubbing the back of his neck. "Now I'm struggling with something I haven't felt before. Fear."

"Michael," Beverly said softly, "why don't you just tell me what you're feeling about Verónica?"

He froze. The glass almost slipped from his hand. His eyes widened. "What—how did you—"

Bev only smiled knowingly. "Because you're my baby brother. I know you better than you know yourself sometimes. Who else would it be?"

Michael blinked, speechless. "I... I haven't told anyone."

"You didn't have to," she replied gently. "I saw it at Thessaly's wedding. I watched you dance with Olivia many times, with other women too, and it was nothing. But with Verónica? Michael, you held her differently. You looked at her differently. I thought maybe it was just that night, but when I saw you again at the gala—I knew. The way you two disappeared the night of the wedding... the way you walked into Dad's the next morning looking like you hadn't slept..."

Michael leaned back, stunned. "And here I thought I was being coy."

"You were," Beverly teased softly. "So coy, you won't even be honest with yourself." She leaned forward, her eyes holding his. "So—how do you feel about her?"

Michael sat in silence, wrestling with the words. Finally, they broke free. "I think... I love her. Like I've loved no one before."

Beverly's smile widened, soft and almost maternal in a way that caught him off guard. "And how does it feel now that you've said it out loud?"

He looked down, then back up, his voice quiet. "It feels honest. Terrifying. But honest. I don't want to hurt her, Bev. I don't know if I'm ready for this. You know how I get with work—how everything else disappears."

"I do," she said. "But I also know how you look when she's in your arms. Michael, I've never seen you so... content. Maybe it's time to make a decision. Not about money, not about deals—God knows you've mastered that. A life decision." She touched his hand. "You always ignore me when I tell you to go to church. But maybe this time, God is your answer. Ask Him."

Michael's throat tightened. He gave a shaky laugh. "You're not holding back tonight, sis."

"Because you need to hear it," she replied. "You're thirty-three. It's time to stop hiding behind business. Look at Anthony—how happy he is. It wasn't long ago that you were both living the same lifestyle. But he grew. You can too."

At the end of the night, as they stood, Michael hugged her tightly. His voice was raw when he said, "I love you, sis. Tonight, you opened my eyes. You made Mom proud."

They held each other, neither rushing to let go.

Michael walked into his apartment, still replaying his conversation with Beverly, her words echoing like a bell. He couldn't be silent. He slipped off his jacket, hung it neatly over the chair, and crossed to the bar. The familiar ritual of pouring a single malt steadied his hands, though it did nothing to quiet his thoughts. He set the glass down, put a record on the turntable, and let Sinatra's smooth voice drift through the room as he sank into the leather couch.

The city lights stretched before him, South Beach glowing in neon, but his eyes weren't on the view. They were on her. Verónica. Every detail of her lingered—her voice, her scent, the way her lips trembled when she whispered his name. Michael felt the weight of realization press down on him. He wasn't just drawn to her. He wasn't just consumed by lust—he was in love with her.

The admission shook him. Why now? Why her? He had built walls high enough to keep out every possibility of this exact thing, and yet she had slipped through, igniting something he thought was long dead. He swirled the amber liquid in his glass, staring into it as though the answer might rise with the ice. Was he truly willing to change his life for her? To risk everything?

Finishing his drink, he turned off the music and walked to his bedroom. Sleep didn't come easily; when it finally did, it was filled with flashes of her smile, the heat of her body, and the sound of her laugh, haunting him even in dreams.

The next morning, Michael arrived at his office still restless, still unsettled. He worked through contracts, meetings, and calls, but the thought of her threaded through everything. Finally, he leaned back in his chair—the decision pressing hard in his chest. He would attend the Delgado, Mercer & Klein Christmas party that Friday. He wasn't sure what would happen—whether he would find the strength to push her away for good, or the honesty to claim her as his.

All he knew was that he needed to see her again. One more time before deciding if he could live with her—or without her.

Chapter 21

Verónica

Verónica sat in her office, freshly back from a long Thanksgiving weekend at her sister Donna's house in Tampa. She hadn't wanted to leave Miami—it felt too much like leaving Michael behind—but she'd forced herself. Maybe the distance would help her clear her mind. The three-and-a-half-hour drive gave her time to process, though each mile felt like another thread pulling her away from him. By the time she reached Donna's driveway, she'd already decided—she was going to tell her sister everything.

Donna had always been her safe haven. A place she could open up without fear of judgment. When Gregory broke her heart, Donna was the one who picked her up. When the marriage finally shattered, it was Donna who reminded her she was strong. Verónica had never spoken Michael's name to her before—not once—but now the secret was too heavy. Donna didn't run in Michael's circles, didn't know Thessaly's people, and that distance gave Verónica comfort. For once, she could speak freely, without fear or reservation.

Wednesday night melted into family chaos—kids laughing, Donna fussing over tomorrow's dinner, the comfort of home wrapping around her like a warm blanket. The next day—Thanksgiving—Verónica was aching with the need to spill everything, her chest tightening every time she thought of him. But Donna's in-laws were everywhere, and she had to wait.

It was Friday night, champagne bottle in hand, when the chance finally came. Donna led her outside, past the pool, to the quiet end of the patio. The kids were asleep; the night air was cool; the bubbles were fizzing in their glasses. Donna leaned back in her chair, eyes sharp with that older-sister knowing.

"So," she said, "what's going on, little sister?"

Verónica let out a long, shaky breath and stared into her glass. "I don't even know where to begin."

"The beginning is usually a good place," Donna teased. They both laughed, but Verónica's heart was pounding.

And then, finally, the words came rushing out. She told Donna about Thessaly's wedding night—how she saw him across the room, how the entire place blurred except for him. The dance, the champagne, the way he looked at her like no man ever had. How she decided, in a wild, reckless moment, to do something she'd never dared before: a one-night stand.

Her voice shook as she told Donna about the way Michael touched her, the way he kissed her. "God, Donna," she whispered, eyes filling, "I've never been kissed like that—or touched like that. I've never felt anything like it. It was the first time I ever... climaxed with a man inside me." Her cheeks burned, but she pressed on. "All those years with Gregory, I thought something was wrong with me. I thought maybe I just couldn't. But with Michael—Donna, he unlocked something in me I didn't even know existed. It was... it was everything. He made me climax over and over with an intensity I never imagined—beyond anything I had known. Now, I just look at him, and I get wet."

Donna reached across the table and squeezed her hand, her eyes soft and full of warmth.

But Verónica wasn't finished. The words poured out faster now—how Michael saved her job, the fire they shared in his office, the way he made her feel like she was walking on the edge of danger every time she was near him. The penthouse overlooking South Beach. The designer clothes he'd had someone buy for her after the gala, as if it were effortless, natural. How she told him she loved him that night, without hesitation, without shame.

"I know it's crazy," Verónica whispered, tears slipping down her cheeks. "I know it's too fast, but Donna, there's no question in my mind. I love him. Just saying his name drives me over the edge. I don't want anyone else. I can't even imagine it."

Donna's laugh broke through the heaviness pressing on Verónica's chest. "Well then, tell him I love him too—for the beautiful expensive shirt, at least." Verónica had bought a shirt for Donna when she went back to the boutique to exchange some clothes Michael had bought for her that didn't fit.

They laughed, but the ache didn't leave Verónica's chest. "I know he cares about me," she said softly. "I know he feels it. But he's so against relationships... I don't know if he'll ever let himself admit it. And I can't stop. I don't want to stop."

She told Donna about Ralph, about the lunch, about how Michael had flown into a rage when he found out. "He told Ralph if he touched me, he was finished," she said, shaking her head in disbelief. "Donna, what does that tell you?"

"That he cares," Donna said firmly. "But, Verónica,"—she squeezed her hand again—"unless he realizes he can't live without you, you'll never truly find happiness. Don't let him drag you down the way Gregory did. Don't let your love blind you. You deserve better than that; you are better than that."

Verónica's lips trembled, her heart pulling in two directions. She wanted to argue, but she knew her sister was right. "I know," she whispered. "I know. But I can't let go. Not yet. I'm giving him as much time as I can." Donna stood up to hug her sister. Verónica wrapped her arms around her sister, squeezing her so tight and said, "I love you."

On the ride back, Verónica spent the entire three and a half hours lost in her thoughts, Donna's words echoing in her mind. For the first time in so long, she had let it all out—every fear, every secret, every piece of her heart that had been caged away for Michael. The release felt like breathing after being held underwater. She could still feel the warmth of Donna's understanding, the way it soothed her wounds without judgment, without pity.

Her chest swelled as she replayed her own confessions. She knew now, with certainty, that what she was feeling for Michael wasn't a passing infatuation or a reckless attraction. It was real—it was deep. It was love that had taken root in her bones, impossible to shake, impossible to deny.

The ache of wanting him was relentless, but there was hope tucked inside it. She didn't need him to be perfect. She didn't even need him to promise forever. All she needed—all she craved—was for him to look at her without restraint, to acknowledge that what burned between them was more than desire. That it was just as undeniable for him as it was for her.

She imagined him finally letting go of his walls and letting her in, envisioning a version of him that held her openly and without hesitation. The thoughts sent a sharp tremor through her—a visceral cocktail of fear and electric anticipation that seemed to hum in time with the engine's vibration. Would it ever actually happen? She kept her eyes fixed on the long, gray winding of the road ahead, her knuckles whitening as she tightened her grip on the steering wheel. It was as if by sheer force of will she could steer her life toward that fragile hope, holding onto the leather rim as though it were the only thing keeping her from drifting away into the "what ifs."

Now, back at the office, only one question consumed her—would Michael show up Friday night at her firm's Christmas party? Would he walk through those doors for her? The thought of it had her pulse racing in ways she couldn't hide, even from herself. She was certain Ralph would come; he had always been too polite not to show up. Javier, without a doubt. And María… yes, María would almost certainly appear, probably for the sole purpose of tossing her little daggers, subtle or not, meant to remind Verónica of her place.

But none of that mattered. Not Ralph's charm, not Javier's presence, not María's petty jabs. All of it fell into the background like meaningless chatter. The only thing that mattered, the only thing her heart and body cared about, was Michael. Would he come? Would he stand across the room and let his eyes search for hers, igniting her with that look that undid her every time? Would he risk being there, knowing how dangerous it was for both of them?

She imagined it over and over—the doors opening, his tall frame filling the space, the shift in the room when he appeared. She could almost feel her knees weaken, her breath stuttering the moment their eyes met. It wasn't just hope that burned inside her—it was need, raw and consuming. And yet, laced through it all was the fear that he wouldn't come at all.

Chapter 22

Verónica

Friday morning, Verónica woke with a restless anticipation that thrummed in her chest. Tonight was the Christmas party at Altura in South Beach—Delgado, Mercer & Klein had rented the entire restaurant, and everyone would be there. The party started at six and would run until ten, which meant there would be no time to rush home and change. What she wore to work would be her armor for the night.

She had chosen carefully. The dress she had bought was for one reason, and one reason only—Michael. Elegant, sensual, but still refined, it was a black wraparound dress that caressed her curves like a lover's hand. Sleeveless and fluid, the fabric whispered with every movement. A slit rode just above her knees, offering teasing glimpses of her legs as if daring someone to want more. With her black four-inch red-soled pumps, her confidence sharpened. She studied her reflection in the mirror, feeling her adrenaline rising. If this didn't get his attention, nothing would.

By afternoon, she felt eyes on her. In the break room, as she poured coffee, Walter sauntered in, his gaze lingering far too long. "God, you look amazing," he said, his grin shameless. "You and me tonight on the dance floor—we'll have them drooling."

Verónica lifted her eyes to him, her tone cool. "I don't think so, Walter. But thank you." She turned on her heel and left, unwilling to let him sour her mood.

At 4:30, as the office buzzed with people leaving early to get to the restaurant before guests arrived, Caroline slipped into her office and shut the door. "Watch yourself tonight, girl. Walter looks like a dog in heat. I heard him telling someone that after a few drinks, he was sure you'd be dancing close to him."

"Fat chance," Verónica replied dryly. "The more he talks to me, the more repulsive I find him."

By six, the restaurant glowed with soft lights and laughter. Servers glided behind trays of delicacies while a four-piece band played a sultry rhythm. Verónica stood with Caroline when Ralph and Javier arrived. She introduced them, smiling politely, trying to hide her nerves. She ate lightly, knowing she would need something in her stomach because the night would be long. Every nerve inside her waited for only one thing. Or rather, one man.

Walter reappeared briefly, all false charm, offering her another glass of champagne and reminding her of a promised dance. She raised her half-full flute and smiled tightly. "I'm fine, thanks." As he walked away, Ralph leaned toward her. "I see you don't like him much."

"Is it that obvious?" she replied, and they both laughed.

But as the hours ticked by, her heart sank. By nine, she knew Michael wasn't coming. Her chest felt hollow, her smile forced. The only comfort was that María hadn't shown up either. She busied herself entertaining Ralph and Javier with Peter at her side, grateful for the buffer against Walter's advances. When Ralph and Javier finally said their goodbyes, Peter raised his glass to her. "Salute. I still don't know how you pulled it off, but you did."

She tried to smile, but the ache inside her deepened. She had dressed for Michael—waited for him. And he hadn't come.

At 9:40, standing at the bar with Peter, her back to the entrance, she felt more tired than she wanted to admit. Peter's eyes suddenly widened, shifting past her shoulder. "Mr. Marino—so glad you could make it."

Verónica froze. Her body knew before she turned. Her pulse thundered in her ears as she spun around and found herself face-to-face with Michael. Every nerve lit up. Her legs trembled, her breath caught.

"Hello, Michael," she managed, her voice hushed.

"Hello, Verónica," he said smoothly, taking her hand. The moment his skin touched hers, electricity jolted through her, sending shivers from her fingertips to her core.

"I'm sorry I'm late," he said, his eyes holding hers with quiet intensity. "I had a prior engagement. I just wanted to stop by to say hello—and to tell you how impressed we've been with your firm's work. Verónica's been a star for us. She's quickly becoming our go-to attorney." He looked at Peter, but his hand lingered in hers, his words sinking directly into her chest. "You'd better be careful. I might just steal her from you."

Peter smiled nervously and said, "I agree. She is truly becoming a star." He then excused himself, sensing Michael wanted to speak with Verónica alone.

She felt as if she were glowing from the inside out.

Walter reappeared, introduced himself, tried to angle in on Michael, and even pitched his tax accounting services. Verónica saw Michael's gaze sharpen, his jaw tightening as he looked at Walter. Walter, oblivious, tried once more to stake his claim. "Verónica, we never had that dance. Brisa's open until two—I could take you there."

Michael's voice cut through, low and commanding. "Verónica's already agreed to have a late dessert with me."

The steel in his tone left no room for argument. Walter faltered, backed down with a weak smile. "Maybe next time." When he extended his hand, Michael hesitated, his jaw tightening before finally obliging.

Alone now, Verónica's pulse raced. The bar was quieter, but between them, the air throbbed with heat. His eyes devoured her. She swallowed hard. "I'm so glad you came," she whispered. "I think Peter already suspects how I landed the Stratus Meridian Group account."

His lips curved into a dangerous smile. "Shall we get out of here?"

She didn't hesitate. "I thought you'd never ask."

Grant was waiting outside. "Good evening, Ms. Verónica," he said as he opened the car door. She slipped inside, Michael close behind. When he asked where she wanted to go, she smiled, her voice soft and daring. "Anywhere you take me."

Michael leaned forward, his voice low but commanding. "Grant, take us to Nocturne."

She had heard of Nocturne before—an exclusive French restaurant perched atop one of Miami's tallest skyscrapers, reserved for the city's elite. From what she could see as they entered, crystal chandeliers spilled soft golden light across the room, and beyond the glass stretched the glittering coastline and the Atlantic.

As they stepped out of the car and approached the building, Verónica's breathing quickened. The thought of being in his world, in his arms again, made her body hum with anticipation. Michael slipped his hand into hers, his grip firm yet gentle, and heat surged straight through her. She tightened her hold, silently begging fate never to make her let go.

As the elevator glided upward, the air seemed to thicken with unspoken promise. Michael turned toward her, his eyes holding her captive. "You look exquisite tonight," he said, his voice low and deliberate. His words wrapped around her, soft and warm, sending a tremor through her.

The doors opened, revealing a breathtaking view from the top floor. The maître d', sharp in his black tuxedo, greeted him with a deference that made it feel as though royalty had arrived. "Good evening, Mr. Marino. I have a perfect table waiting for you." Michael nodded, guiding her forward with a hand at the small of her back, his touch igniting sparks that danced beneath her skin.

They sat, and almost instantly the champagne arrived—rose-colored bubbles rising with elegance, promising decadence. Michael leaned closer, his gaze never leaving hers. "What do you feel like having?" he asked.

She stared at him, heart racing, lips trembling with honesty. "You."

His slow smile unraveled her. He leaned over and pressed the softest kiss against her lips, one that lingered just long enough to make her ache for more. "You will," he murmured, and those two words alone set her whole body aflame.

Plates came and went, though food was the last thing on her mind. Michael ordered Beluga caviar, served on sculpted blue ice so striking it looked like art. She had never tasted it before; the briny richness against her tongue was new, indulgent. "It's supposed to be a powerful aphrodisiac," he whispered, his eyes glinting with mischief.

She leaned in, lips brushing close to his ear, daring herself. "I have my aphrodisiac sitting right next to me."

His soft chuckle curled inside her, followed by another tender kiss, one that promised storms yet to come. Dessert followed—rich layers of chocolate on chocolate, bittersweet and sinful. Even that couldn't compete with the hunger curling tighter inside her with each passing second.

By the time the clock neared midnight, her body was alive with nervous energy. Michael reached for her hand once more, and she rose without hesitation, every nerve sparking at his touch. They walked to the elevator together, hand in hand, and she knew—tonight was only just beginning.

Chapter 23

Verónica

As the elevator doors slid open to his penthouse, Verónica's chest tightened with excitement. The anticipation thrummed in her chest like a drumbeat. Michael barely gave her time to step inside before he turned her around, his lips crashing onto hers. He kissed her so deeply, so passionately, that her knees weakened. When he finally pulled back, his eyes burned into hers.

"I've missed you," he whispered.

The words melted her, but his kiss had already said it all. The fact that he hadn't rushed her straight here but had taken her out—proudly walking her on his arm, showing her to the world, treating her like she was his queen—touched her more deeply than words ever could.

He led her by the hand into the bedroom, his jacket still on, his kisses insatiable. Desire rolled off him in waves, making her skin flush with heat. Her head spun—half of her floating on a cloud, the other half desperate to rip away every barrier between them. When his fingers pulled the tie on her wrap dress, it fell open. She gently shook her shoulders, and the dress slipped down and pooled on the floor. She stood there in nothing but a black thong and heels, quivering with hunger for him.

Michael froze, taking her in. His eyes roamed every inch of her bare skin, and a slow smile spread across his face.

"God... you're gorgeous."

She tore at his tie with eager hands, her fingers fumbling against the buttons of his shirt, desperate to free him. His belt came undone, the sound of the buckle fueling the fire between them, and his pants slid to the floor, pooling with his shirt and tie beside her discarded dress. He pulled her in close, skin to skin, the heat of his body enveloping her. Pressed flush against him, she couldn't ignore the rigid evidence of his desire. The heavy, unyielding heat of him strained against the dark fabric of his underwear, a hard promise that sent a fresh jolt of electricity straight to her core. With two steady steps, he guided her back onto the bed, holding her tight as if he couldn't bear to let go. His kisses crashed into hers, deep and consuming, igniting every nerve until her lips burned with the hunger she could no longer hide.

His mouth trailed down Verónica's neck, each kiss searing, each lick and nip leaving her breathless. When he reached her breasts, his hands caressed while his lips teased, licking, sucking, tugging until her nipples felt hard like small pebbles, aching points of pleasure. Her moans spilled into the air, louder, more desperate, as if she were unraveling beneath him. His kisses descended lower, across her stomach, until he reached the thin barrier of her thong, damp with need. His fingers slipped it off, teasing, tormenting, until his tongue found her lower lips. The sensation jolted her into low cries that turned into frantic, helpless screams.

She tried to tug him up, clutching at his hair, her voice broken with urgency. "Michael... you're driving me insane. Please, I need you inside me."

But he only smiled against her skin, his voice low, teasing, commanding. "Not yet, gorgeous. I'm not finished."

He seemed determined to keep her on edge, moving away from her center to slide lower, lifting her leg, kissing down to her ankle. He slipped off her heel, his lips lingering at her foot, then curling around each toe with a devotion that sent shock-waves of sensation through her. She gasped, half in disbelief, half in wild pleasure, unable to stop her moans. By the time he worked his way up her other leg and returned to her soaked center, she was trembling, undone, begging for release. His mouth closed over her again, his tongue circling her sweet spot, sucking, stroking with maddening precision until she lost all control. Her hips bucked against him, her voice shattered into cries of his name—Michael, oh my God, Michael—as ecstasy ripped through her, leaving her body shaking, her heart pounding, her legs weak.

He held her, steadying her as the waves subsided, his gaze intense and unwavering. When he finally looked up, he met her eyes. She looked at him and whispered, "I love you so much, Michael. I just can't believe what you do to my body. Please don't ever stop." He climbed up and met her lips, kissing her passionately. He brought his fingers to his lips, tasting her again, a dangerous smirk playing at his mouth. "You taste incredible."

The sight made her body quiver all over again. She pulled him to her, crushing her lips against his; the kiss deep, penetrating, almost frantic.

When their mouths broke apart, his voice was ragged. "Relax for a moment. I'm not done with you yet."

She cupped his face, her words fluttering with desire. "You'd better not be. I need to feel you inside me, Michael." She had never wanted anyone the way she wanted him now.

They tangled together again, whispering half-coherent words, sweet nothings blending with the pulse of their hunger. She pressed kisses along his neck, down his chest, savoring the heat of his skin beneath her lips. Her mouth found his hardened nipples, teasing them before trailing lower, lower, until she reached his abs. Her hands tugged his underwear down, freeing him, and the sight of his erection made her shiver with both awe and anticipation.

She wrapped her fingers around him, stroking slowly before lowering her mouth over his length. Her tongue slid along his tip, her lips tightening as she took him in deeper, savoring his taste, the sound of his low moans spurring her on. His body twitched, harder, thicker, until his breath turned ragged and his voice broke. "Verónica... stop. Come up here. I need to be inside you."

He tore open a condom, thrusting it into her hand, and she rolled it over him with deliberate care, trembling with anticipation. Then she straddled him, guiding him against her slick heat before sliding down slowly, inch by inch, until he was buried deep inside her. A cry tore from her throat, raw and unrestrained. The stretch, the fullness—it was overwhelming, intoxicating. She straightened, riding him, moving in rhythm as his hands captured her breasts, teasing her nipples until she was writhing, screaming again, consumed by another climax when his manhood touched that spot inside her she never knew existed. It left her gasping, shaking above him.

Michael's movements suddenly turned fierce. With a growl, he flipped her onto her back, thrusting hard, driving into her with wild abandon. His body tensed, his breath broke, and with a last cry, he exploded inside her, his body collapsing over hers as if he could merge them into one.

He held her there, their bodies tangled, his weight grounding her in the sweetest bliss she had ever known. Her eyes closed, and for a long moment, nothing existed but the sound of their breath and the echo of the storm they had unleashed. She was in bliss beyond her wildest dreams.

They fell asleep in each other's arms, wrapped in warmth that made her feel safe and loved. When her eyes fluttered open, she found Michael already awake, watching her with that quiet smile that melted everything inside her. His arms were still around her, protective and possessive, as if he were anchoring her to the bed and refused to let her drift away.

"Good morning, beautiful," he whispered.

Her heart leapt, a rush of heat spreading through her. She smiled, her voice soft with emotion as she whispered back, "I love you, Michael."

His arms tightened around her, his eyes dark with something she couldn't name. "As much as I want to kiss every inch of your body again right now," he murmured, "I think we should get up, shower, get dressed, and go out for breakfast."

Michael's sudden suggestion that they go out for breakfast instead of slipping back beneath the sheets and having a repeat of last night caught Verónica completely off guard. Waking and looking at him—hair tousled, no clothes, just a sheet up to his waist—devastatingly handsome; it sent a fresh rush of desire through her. She felt the moisture between her legs, her skin warming all over again, yet he seemed perfectly composed, his focus already shifting toward the world outside their bedroom door.

A knot tightened in her stomach as uncertainty crept in. Why didn't he seem to feel it, too? He always had before. Doubt slipped in, quiet but sharp, whispering questions she didn't want to face. Was this his gentle way of creating distance? Had the fire that burned hot between them cooled? Maybe she had pushed too hard, felt too deeply, wanted too much. Or worse—perhaps she simply wasn't enough. A hundred doubts screamed in her head.

Still, she refused to let those fears show. Drawing a slow breath, she forced a smile. "Okay. I guess I can have breakfast in my dress, at least it's not a gown."

He laughed, low and warm. "You looked amazing in that dress last night. As much as I'd love to see it on you again, go into my closet and turn left."

She frowned, puzzled, but he only smirked. "Just go. You'll see."

She slipped out of bed, bare, unashamed. He had erased that old insecurity, convincing her she was beautiful even without clothes. His gaze lingered on her as she crossed the room, and she let him look—no, she wanted him to. She slid the closet door open, lights flickering on, and her breath caught. It wasn't just a closet. It was a boutique. Rows of women's clothing, shoes, dresses, lingerie—an entire section dedicated to her. All brand-new, every piece in her size.

A shocked cry burst out of her. "I don't understand!" She snatched a long T-shirt, pulled it over her head, and hurried back out. He was lying on the bed, one arm propped, watching her with a look of pure satisfaction as he drank in the shock on her face.

"You're crazy," she blurted, her heart pounding. "How—when—why?"

He looked at her with a tenderness that made her chest tighten. "I knew when I decided to go to the Christmas party, we'd end up here. I didn't know what we'd be doing today, so I made sure you'd have choices."

Her chest ached, overwhelmed. No one had ever treated her like this. No one had ever thought ahead for her or cared for her in this way. Tears stung her eyes as she threw herself into his arms. "No one has ever treated me like you do."

He kissed her hair and murmured, "Then let's shower and get breakfast."

She tilted her head back, giving him a wicked smile. "Are you sure? We have time."

His eyes darkened, desire flickering. He groaned, "Hurry up before I change my mind."

She walked into the bathroom, brushing her teeth before stepping into the shower. The water was hot against her skin, but she still shivered when she felt his eyes on her. He came in, brushed his teeth, looked at her through the clear glass, and then walked over and stepped under the spray. The steam wrapped around them as his arms slid around her waist.

He kissed her slowly at first, then deeper, and her body melted. His lips trailed down her neck, her breasts, worshiping her. "I know I said we shouldn't," he growled against her skin, "but your body is too irresistible. I can't be near you without wanting all of you."

His mouth claimed her, moving lower, lower, until he was on his knees before her. Heat shot through her veins as his tongue found her, teasing, circling, tasting. The mix of water and the flood of her desire left her trembling, desperate, and undone. Her moans grew louder, echoing off the tiles, until she braced herself on the bench, lifting her leg, giving him full access. The pleasure ripped through her like fire—her scream muffled by the steam, her body shattering around his tongue.

Her legs wobbled, barely holding her, but he rose, kissed her, then spun her gently to face the wall. His body pressed against hers, hard, urgent, relentless. When he slid into her from behind, she gasped, the rhythm fierce, passionate, unstoppable. Each thrust made her cry out, clawing at the marble, surrendering everything. Just as his rhythm reached a frantic peak, he suddenly pulled away, his breath ragged and his body tense.

She dropped to her knees, taking him into her mouth, greedy, determined to finish what he'd started. His hands tangled in her hair, his moans filling the shower until he erupted, hot and fierce, and she swallowed every drop, not letting go until he sagged against the wall, undone.

When she stood, he pulled her into his arms, kissed her softly, lingering against her lips. His voice was hoarse. "You are beyond words, Verónica. No one—no one—makes me feel like you do."

Those words struck deeper than any climax, setting her heart ablaze. For the first time, she knew, truly knew, how wrong Gregory had been all those years. Michael's words drowned out every cruel whisper of the past. With him, she wasn't broken. She wasn't lacking. She was everything.

Chapter 24
Michael

After the shower, they dressed. Verónica chose pink shorts, light cream sneakers, and a white T-shirt knotted at the side. The soft cotton clung just enough to reveal the perfect shape of her full C-cup curves, the bra beneath leaving no doubt of her beauty. When she stepped out of the bathroom, her hair tied back casually, she looked effortless—fresh, radiant, innocent. Michael stared at her, breath catching. God, she looked amazing. So pure, so real. And yet, she was also temptation incarnate. How could he not know—right here, right now—that this was what he wanted for the rest of his life?

He tugged on jeans, a shirt, and red driving shoes. They left the apartment hand in hand, and he gripped her fingers tighter than he meant to, as if letting go even for a second would risk losing her. His mind kept circling the same questions. What was he supposed to say to her? How could he make her understand the storm inside him? Beverly's words had given him clarity, but the clarity faded quickly when fear crept in—fear of hurting Verónica, fear of making a mistake, fear of committing and then failing her.

They walked a few blocks through the South Beach salty air until they found a quiet little neighborhood spot for brunch. She sat across from him, sunlight spilling through the window. She tilted her head, studying him. "Michael," she said softly, "I know something is on your mind. I can tell."

He gave her a crooked smile. "See? Now you can read me too." She laughed lightly, but her eyes didn't leave his.

He exhaled slowly. "Verónica... this is so hard. I don't even know where to begin. You know there's something between us—something deep, powerful. The chemistry is insane. I've never felt this with anyone else. When I'm with you, like last night, like this morning...it's like the world disappears. It's only us. And then I look at my brothers and my sister. I see how content they are, how they smile with their spouses, how Anthony nearly burst with joy when he found out Angela was pregnant. And I wonder—why can't I have that? Why is it so hard for me? Was I broken somewhere along the way?"

Her hand slid over his, her thumb brushing gently. Her voice was steady, but her eyes shimmered. "Michael, you are all I want. All I need. I never knew actual love until you. I can't explain it either, but I know it's real—I don't want to lose you... But you have to decide. You can't keep me dangling between your fear and your desire."

He swallowed hard, her words cutting sharper than any knife. "And this is why I told you not to love me. Because I struggle with relationships. Because I don't even understand myself half the time. You would be smart to walk away now—save yourself. Maybe I'm not the man who can think about forever."

Her eyes flashed then—not sadness, but defiance. She leaned in, grip tightening on his hand. "Michael, do you really expect me to just walk away? To forget how I feel when I'm with you? To erase what you do to me when you touch me, when you make love to me?" Her voice quivered, not with weakness, but with fire. "How do you expect me to un-feel that? How do you expect me to pretend it never happened?"

For the first time, it wasn't him leading—it was her. Verónica wasn't begging. She was claiming.

Her words caught him off guard, sharp and undeniable, piercing through the walls he had built around himself. She was right. He needed to figure it out—figure himself out.

After brunch, they walked back to his building. Grant was already waiting with the car, but Michael waved him off. "You can go, Grant. I'll drive her home." Verónica's face lit with surprise and excitement. Grant nodded and departed, while Michael took her hand and guided her toward the garage. They climbed into his Ferrari, and the moment the engine roared to life, the charged silence between them returned as they reflected on their heavy conversation at breakfast.

He dropped the top, letting the sunlight pour in as they pulled out into the street. At a red light, he glanced at her. The way the sun brushed across her face, catching the softness of her lips, the light in her hair—it was too much. Without thinking, he took out his phone and snapped a picture.

"You look gorgeous," he told her, his voice low and reverent. "I want to save this picture."

She smiled, not coy, not shy, but with the confidence that told him she knew exactly what she was doing to him. Her fingers slid into his, warm, sure, claiming him without a word.

When they pulled in front of her building, he cut the engine but didn't move. The silence stretched until she broke it. "Would you like to come up?"

God, yes. Every part of him screamed yes. But he forced himself to shake his head. "I would love to," he said quietly, "but I'm not going to. I need some time to process things—I had the most wonderful time with you—don't forget that."

She gave him a small, knowing smile. "Not a chance."

Then she leaned in, kissing him softly, her lips pressing to his with a promise, with intent. She didn't rush, didn't beg—it was measured, controlled, deliberate. He knew she was telling him she knew what she wanted, and what she wanted was him.

When she pulled back, he whispered, "I think it's time we exchanged numbers. Just in case we need to say something."

He smiled, teasing. "I already have yours."

She smiled. "How's that? I never gave it to you."

"No, you didn't. But I got it from Grant—the night you called him after the gala."

Her eyes widened, recognition flashing in them, but before she could respond, he texted her, so she'd have his. "Now you have my number," he said. "I almost called you that day. I wanted to. But... I reamed Ralph out instead."

Her lips curved as though she already knew. He sighed. "I need to apologize to him. But not yet. I wasn't angry at him—I was angry at myself."

She squeezed his hand gently, her eyes softening. "I have a feeling you'll figure it out. I'll say a prayer that you do."

He chuckled, shaking his head. "Now you sound like Beverly, with her prayers and church."

Verónica gave him a sly little smile. "Don't knock it until you try it."

She opened the door, stepped out, then turned back to him, her voice steady, her eyes burning into his. "I love you."

The words hit him like a punch to the chest, leaving him breathless. He wanted to follow her, take her in his arms, tell her he loved her too, and never let her go. But he sat there, gripping the wheel, watching her disappear into the building. His heart screamed after her, but he couldn't move.

He knew he needed time to think and figure things out.

Chapter 25
Michael

Two weeks had passed since Michael dropped Verónica off at home. He threw himself into work as a distraction, burying his thoughts beneath endless contracts, marketing plans, and meetings. Every morning, he rose at five and was at the gym by six, disciplined and focused—or at least trying to be. Yet each time he walked into his closet, his eyes betrayed him. They lingered on the rows of clothes hanging neatly on the left side—the ones he had bought for her, waiting for her. He couldn't bring himself to touch them, couldn't bring himself to remove them. A part of him decided that the pain of seeing them every day was necessary—punishment or reminder, he wasn't sure which.

By Monday morning, he leaned back in his chair, his jaw tight. How long am I going to torture myself? The truth pressed on him like a weight he could no longer deny. He wanted her. Needed her. He didn't want to lose her. And yet he kept sabotaging the one thing that made him feel alive. He promised himself he'd put the thoughts aside, at least until tonight, when he could think and unravel privately.

The sharp buzz of his phone shattered the silence. Beverly's name flashed across the screen. He answered on the first ring.

"Wow, early for you, sis."

Her voice was tight, clipped. "Michael... It's Verónica. She's in the hospital."

His stomach dropped, and shock was immediate. "What?" His voice boomed through the office. "Where? What happened? Is she okay?"

"I don't know everything yet," Beverly admitted quickly. "One of my AUSAs called me. Apparently, Verónica was involved in a scuffle with someone from her office last night. At first, they thought it might have been a mugging, but the details are still sketchy."

Michael frowned. "How would someone from her office have anything to do with a criminal investigation?"

Beverly sighed softly. "Agents from my office, who were already surveilling the man accused of the attack, informed me. He's the brother of someone connected to a major case I'm working on. When Verónica's name came up as the possible victim, I thought you'd want to know."

Michael's entire body locked with rage and fear. "Of course I want to know. I want to know everything you find out. What hospital is she in?"

"Mount Sinai Medical Center."

"I'm on my way," he snapped, already grabbing his jacket. "Keep me posted. Every detail."

He slammed the off and grabbed the desk phone. "Sara, cancel everything. All meetings. Now." Without waiting, he called Grant. "Car. Out front. Now."

By the time Sara appeared in the doorway, he was already striding past her. Outside, Grant had the SUV waiting, the door open. Michael climbed in, his voice like a blade. "Mount Sinai. Fast."

Red lights blurred past, horns blared as Grant threaded the car through traffic. Ten minutes later, Michael stormed through the hospital doors, demanding, "Verónica Liora. What room?"

The receptionist hesitated. "I'm sorry, sir, visiting hours—"

Michael's cell was already at his ear. "Lieutenant, I need you at Mount Sinai Medical Center. Now."

Within minutes, his contact arrived, flashing his badge. Together, they pushed past restrictions until Michael heard the words: "They are just bringing her to room 1340A."

Michael reached the doorway just as they wheeled her in. The sight punched the air out of his lungs. Bruised. Fragile. His unshakable, fiery Verónica looked broken—and it gutted him.

Her swollen eye fluttered open. She looked up, and there he was. Tears welled as she whispered, "I'm so sorry... I didn't want you to see me like this. Look at me, I'm a mess."

Michael dropped beside her, his voice low and raw. "Hey. You look gorgeous. And there's nowhere else I'd rather be."

The nurses moved him aside, and for the first time in years, Michael felt powerless. He stepped out, jumped on his phone, and called in favors. By the hour's end, Verónica was in the hospital's presidential suite, guarded by two private nurses.

She drifted in and out of the painkillers they gave her, but each time her hand sought his. He stayed at her bedside, whispering softly, promising silently. Never again—never leaving. Never letting her go.

When Beverly called back, he answered immediately.

"How is she?" she asked.

"She's stable, looks beat up, but I think she is going to be fine," Michael said. "Private room. I'm waiting for the doctor."

"Good. Now, listen to me." Beverly's voice was stern, warning. "Don't turn into Vincent on me."

Michael's jaw tightened. He said nothing, only listened.

"The guy she had the altercation with was Walter Brennan," Beverly continued. "You know him?"

Michael's voice was ice. "I met the scumbag."

"Well, the police took him in, but they released him when no one could testify that he actually attacked her. His story was that he'd been drunk—that she'd been coming on to him all night, and when she slipped into the ladies' room, he followed. He told them he thought she wanted him to kiss her. That's when he stumbled, so drunk he couldn't even keep his balance. He claimed he fell on top of her by accident, which is what caused her broken arm, her face hitting the tile, and the bruises."

The words hung heavy in the air, each one twisting like a blade.

"Several witnesses confirmed he was sloppy drunk," Bev continued, clipped and bitter. "The ASA in Miami said it wasn't enough to charge him with a felony. At best, a misdemeanor—but they decided not to press charges. When others came in and saw him on top of her on the floor, he was full of apologies, stumbling over himself. They called the ambulance for her, and... here we are."

Michael said nothing. His silence said everything.

The doctor arrived soon after, detailing her injuries.

"A slight break in her right arm below the elbow. We set it. Contusions were mostly on her face from hitting the floor, along with a slight concussion. Other than that, she was very lucky. We will keep her for a day or two just to make sure the concussion has cleared. In a few days, the bruises will start to disappear. She'll recover and be fine."

Michael asked, "Was she raped?"

"No evidence of rape, therefore we didn't do a test for it." Relief slammed through him, though fury still churned.

When they left, Michael returned to her bedside. She stirred, eyes glassy but aware.

"Can you hear me?" he whispered.

Her lips trembled into the faintest smile. "Yes."

He cupped her face, a voice rough with emotion. "I love you, Verónica. I'm never going to let you go."

Her tears slipped silently down her cheeks. She clutched his hand with surprising strength. "If this is what it took to make you realize that, then it was worth every bit of pain I feel."

He bent, kissed her, sealing the vow. "Rest. I'm here. And I'm not going anywhere."

Early evening, Beverly walked in. Verónica was still sleeping, her face pale against the hospital pillow, while Michael sat on one couch with Anthony, who had only just arrived. Beverly's eyes went to Verónica immediately, and her shoulders eased with relief.

"I know she looks bad," she whispered, "but thank God she's going to be fine." Her gaze shifted to her brother. "Michael."

Michael gave a small nod, his jaw tight. Beverly came over, sat between her brothers, and reached for Michael's hand.

"I can see it in your face," she said softly, "this unfortunate episode cleared your dilemma."

Michael's lips curved into the faintest smile, his head dipping once.

Beverly's voice grew firmer. "I'm going to say this again to both of you. You've built an enormous business, supporting hundreds—probably thousands—of people. I don't want you," she looked directly at Michael, "doing anything foolish to jeopardize it. I know it's in your blood, but let the police handle this. Please."

Anthony nodded in agreement. Michael, however, remained silent.

"Michael, do you hear me?" Beverly pressed.

"I hear you, sis," he replied at last, voice even.

But deep down, Michael knew he couldn't let this go. Now that he had found the love of his life, there was no chance he would allow some scumbag to get away with hurting her. For the moment, though, he buried the thought, shoving it to the back burner. His focus was only on Verónica—getting her healthy, keeping her safe.

For the next two days, Michael barely left her side. He slept in the hospital suite, refusing to go home even when Verónica begged him to.

"Please, Michael, go rest in your own bed," she whispered more than once, but he only shook his head. He called Sara and told her to cancel his entire schedule until further notice. Work could wait. She couldn't.

On Thursday, Michael finally brought her home—not to her place but to his. A nurse stayed in the guest room, despite Verónica's insistence that she didn't need one.

"Michael," she said gently one afternoon, "I need to go to my apartment to pick up some things."

He frowned, immediately shaking his head. "Make a list. I'll have Grant get whatever you need."

Verónica laughed softly, that warm, sexy laugh that always undid him. "I have some personal things I don't want Grant to get. I need to go."

Michael sighed, conceding, but his protective edge never wavered. "Fine. Then we'll all go. You get what you need, but you're not lifting a finger."

She smiled at him, kissed him lightly on the lips, and whispered, "I love you."

This time, there was no doubt, no hesitation to hold him back. Michael let the words out, his voice low and steady. "I love you too."

The effect was instantaneous. He felt a sharp, sudden tremor run through her, followed by a long, shaky exhale that seemed to carry away months of built-up tension. She didn't just hug him; she anchored herself to him, burying her face against the crook of his neck as her body went soft in his arms.

Michael pulled her closer, his hands tangling in her hair, savoring the way she finally seemed to settle into his embrace. He could feel the rapid, joyous thud of her heart against his own—a frantic, rhythmic pounding he could feel through his shirt. It was the feeling of a woman finally letting go of her armor, of a barrier between them finally crumbling.

He leaned his head against hers, breathing her in, aware that the weight of the silence had been replaced by something solid and undeniable. The words were out, hanging in the air like a promise, and as she clung to him, Michael knew he had finally given her the one thing she had been too afraid to hope for.

Michael gently guided her as she packed what she needed. He refused to let her carry anything, repeating the doctor's orders like a mantra. "No heavy exercise. You're supposed to rest."

She smiled only, letting him fuss over her.

It wasn't just about keeping her safe anymore, and Michael could feel that realization humming in the small space between them. His protectiveness had shifted into something deeper—something fierce and unyielding that he could no longer label as mere responsibility. It was love, raw and absolute, and in the way she looked at him, he knew she finally recognized it too.

Inside, Michael gathered everything into one pile in the living room. Then Grant came up and carried the boxes and bags down to the car. Verónica waited, watching through the window. Michael could see her face glow at the sight of him hauling her life into his.

Saturday night, Verónica was feeling stronger. Dinner had been brought in, and after they ate, they curled up on the couch, her head resting against his chest, his arms wrapped securely around her. They watched a movie, but neither of them was really paying attention. Every brush of his fingertips against her arm, every stolen glance at her lips, only fueled the fire smoldering between them.

When it was finally bedtime, Verónica slipped into the bathroom. Michael stretched out across the bed, waiting, thinking she would return in her usual soft pajamas. But when the door opened, his breath caught. She stepped out wearing a black negligee, sheer silk that clung to her curves and left little to the imagination. The bruises on her face were fading, but her right eye—bright, determined, burning—stole his attention completely.

"God, have I missed you," he murmured, sitting up, his voice hoarse. "Are you sure you're ready for this?"

She gave him a slow, sensual smile. "Michael," she whispered, walking to him with deliberate grace, "I don't just want this—I need it. I need to feel you. I need to take back what was stolen from me."

He reached for her, but she caught his hand and pressed it against her heart. "No more gentle, wounded looks. Don't look at me like I'm broken. I'm not. I want you to see me—want me—exactly as I am."

Her boldness stirred something deep inside him. He nodded, his eyes locked on hers. "Then show me," he said softly.

She climbed onto the bed, straddling him, her silk brushing against his bare skin. His hands instinctively went to her waist, sliding up to her breasts. Michael gently squeezed her nipples between his fingers, and she moaned. "Tonight, Michael," she whispered, lowering her lips to his neck, "I'm in control."

Her kisses trailed from his throat to his chest, slowly, teasing, deliberate. He groaned, his muscles tightening under her touch. She slid lower, tugging at the waistband of his shorts, her lips pressing into the hard planes of his stomach. He reached down, trying to guide her, but she slapped his hand playfully away with one hand. "Patience," she breathed, her voice dripping with seduction.

By the time she slid back up to meet his mouth, his self-control was unraveling. Her kiss was fierce, devouring, and when she smiled at him, his hands tore the negligee open, desperate for her.

Their bodies tangled, her nails scraping lightly across his shoulders as she whispered in his ear, "I want to feel you inside me. Now."

Michael fumbled for the drawer, pulled out a condom, tore it open, but before he could roll it on, she took it from him. With a steady hand, she rolled it onto him herself, her eyes locked on his, a daring smile curving her lips. "Mine," she said simply, and lowered herself onto him in one slow, claiming motion.

His groan was guttural, almost primal, as she moved, her rhythm purposeful, commanding. He let her set the pace, let her ride him, her body owning every thrust. Her moans filled the room, raw and unrestrained, each one pulling him closer to the edge.

Michael finally gripped her hips, meeting her thrusts, his body unable to hold back. "Verónica," he gasped, his voice breaking, "I can't—"

"Then don't," she whispered fiercely, pressing her forehead to his. "Lose control for me."

And he did. With one final, desperate surge, he exploded, his body shaking beneath her as he held her close, his arms locking her to him as if he'd never let go.

She collapsed against his chest, both of them gasping, trembling. He kissed her hair, his voice ragged with apology. "I'm sorry... I couldn't wait for you. I just—"

She lifted her head, silencing him with a kiss that stole his breath. "Never apologize for wanting me," she whispered against his lips. "I love you, Michael. All of you. Even the part that loses control."

He smiled through the haze of passion, his hand cradling her face. "God, I love you too."

Chapter 26
Verónica

When Verónica's eyes opened Sunday morning, Michael was lying beside her, just staring. His gaze was soft, almost reverent, as if he couldn't believe she was real. Their legs still touched, a quiet reminder of the night before, and her heart swelled with a joy she used to only dream about as a girl.

"What time is it?" she whispered, reluctant to disturb the magic of the moment.

"Eight-thirty," he said with a smile.

"I can't believe I slept so late." She stretched, torn between wanting to stay wrapped up in him and the pull of her Sunday routine. "I'd love to lie here with you, but I need to shower. You know, ten o'clock Mass."

"I know." His grin deepened. "Let's shower quickly and get dressed."

She frowned at him playfully. "Why are you showering so early? You don't have to be at your dad's until later."

Michael's expression softened, and his voice lowered, steady and certain. "There's no more 'I.' It's us now. I'm coming to church with you. After all, between you and Beverly telling me how wonderful it is, I figured I'd better try it."

For a moment, she couldn't breathe. Her chest filled with something indescribable, bursting with joy that shimmered straight to her soul. She threw her arms around him and clung to him as if she never wanted to let go. "Michael, you're a dream. I love you so much."

His hand cupped her face, thumb brushing her cheek as he whispered, "I love you too—and it feels so damn good to finally say it."

Tears pricked her eyes, but she blinked them back, too happy to let them fall.

"After church, we'll grab a light breakfast," he continued, "and then we're going to my dad's for Sunday dinner with the family."

Her eyes widened. "You mean...you want to bring me to a family dinner?"

He smiled that devilishly confident smile, but softer now, more intimate. "They'd be upset if I didn't go. And I'm not going without you. So yes, I want to bring you. It's time I showed you off."

Her heart bubbled over. He wanted her—not in secret, not behind closed doors—but truly wanted her, all of her, in every part of his life. She hugged him tightly, whispering against his ear, "We need to go, or we'll be late for mass. Otherwise, I'd take you on that bed and make love to you again and again."

He laughed, the sound deep and rich, kissing her hard before pulling back. "I'll take a rain check."

"Deal," she teased, still breathless.

They showered together, his hands brushing hers under the warm spray, small touches that burned with unspoken promises. By 9:30, they were out the door. Michael insisted on driving, telling Grant to take the day off. His driver offered a quick, appreciative smile and a nod, but it was Verónica who felt like the lucky one when Michael opened the passenger door of his Ferrari for her.

"Okay, where are we going?" he asked as he slid behind the wheel.

"Our Lady of Grace in Brickell."

He nodded, shifting gears smoothly, the engine's hum filling the silence between them. She recalled him telling her about growing up Catholic in a traditional Italian family, even though he'd admitted he hadn't set foot in a church since he was sixteen. Still, when they walked inside and found their seats, something about the way he carried himself felt...natural. Like he belonged.

During the Mass, her connection to him felt distinct, different, surpassing mere passion or love. It felt sacred. Like God Himself was whispering in her ear, This is the one I made for you.

Every so often, she squeezed Michael's hand tight, unable to hold back the tide of emotion. Each time, he squeezed back, smiling faintly, grounding her. When they walked forward to receive communion together, she thought her heart might burst. For the first time in her life, she didn't just feel like she belonged to someone—she felt like they belonged to something greater.

After Mass, he slipped his arm around her waist and said quietly, "Want to hear something strange? That was the first time I had received communion since I was sixteen. And it felt...natural. Like I never missed a week all these years."

She smiled, her throat thick with emotion. "Maybe God's telling you something."

He chuckled softly. "Maybe."

They grabbed a light breakfast and then headed to his dad's house. The closer they got, the more the nerves inside her twisted. Her palms grew damp, her stomach fluttering with butterflies that were equal parts excitement and fear. Meeting his family in this setting—it wasn't just another step. It was everything.

Michael glanced at her, noticing her silence. "Hey, relax. You look gorgeous. They're going to love you almost as much as I do." He leaned in at a red light and kissed her gently, so tenderly her nerves melted for just a moment.

As they pulled up to the house, got out, and walked hand in hand, she prayed he was right.

They walked in, and everyone was already gathered, laughter and voices filling the air. Beverly was the first to reach her. She wrapped her arms around her with such warmth that it nearly stole her breath. "I knew it," she whispered against her ear, her voice thick with certainty. "The very first time I saw him dance with you at Thessaly's wedding, I knew. I'm so glad he found you."

Her chest swelled, tears pressing hot against her eyes. She tried to blink them back, but the love in Beverly's words bubbled through her, loosening something she hadn't even realized was still bound inside. Beverly took her hand and smiled, eyes glinting with mischief and truth. "Come," she said. "Let me introduce you to everyone."

She led her around the room, hand warm against hers, her presence steadying her as she guided her from one embrace to the next. His family welcomed her as if she had always been there, as if her place among them had long been reserved. In the kitchen, his father looked up from where he was stirring a simmering sauce. Wiping his hands on a dishtowel, he crossed the room with a grin that melted the last of her nerves. "It's so wonderful to finally meet you," he said, his eyes kind, his tone carrying the weight of something more. "I've heard so much about you."

She glanced at Beverly, startled, and Beverly only smiled knowingly. "I knew all along you'd be here," she said with conviction. "I just didn't know when." They both laughed, but her words lodged deep inside her, filling her with both wonder and a trembling sense of destiny.

The family swept her into their warmth, their stories, their laughter. It was joyously overwhelming—every smile, every question, every hug felt like a thread weaving her into the very fabric of their family. For the first time in years, she felt what she had longed for in silence: belonging. A home. Not just through Michael, but through all of them.

By the time the clock crept close to ten, Michael gently touched her arm. "I think it's time," he said with that steady authority of his. "Verónica's supposed to take it easy. She needs her rest." His words were practical, protective—but when his eyes slid over her, she knew. He wasn't just thinking about her rest. He was thinking about the rain check she had promised him, and the promise shimmered in the air between them like a secret only they shared. Her skin flushed at the thought.

As they said their goodbyes, her heart swelled again at how they had embraced her. Their love echoed the way Michael had shown love to her while she lay in the hospital. She remembered that first day, when he asked for Donna's number, how he had called her himself, his voice calm but firm as she panicked on the other end of the line. He told her she was fine, assured her, soothed her, then, with that same take-charge tone that always made her feel safe, said: "Why don't you come see for yourself?" When she confessed her car troubles, he didn't hesitate. "I'm sending a car. Just tell me the address." And when she protested, he'd simply said, "Please don't let him come back empty." That was Michael—decisive, unshakable, quietly tender beneath the steel.

On the way home, Michael glanced at her, his hands steady on the wheel, his tone softer than usual. "You're quiet. Were they too much tonight?"

She shook her head quickly. "Oh, no. Not at all. I loved them. I can't believe how wonderful they made me feel." And it was true—his family had wrapped her in warmth, acceptance, and laughter. But her silence wasn't about them.

"Then what's up?" he pressed gently. His voice was calm, but she felt exposed under the weight of his curiosity. It felt as though he could already read the smallest shift in her expression, making it impossible to hide. He knew her too well, could read the smallest shift in her expression. She tried to hide behind a smile, but the heat in her cheeks betrayed her.

"Verónica," he said, voice low and steady, "I know you. Something's on your mind."

She drew a long breath, steadying herself. The words sat heavily on her chest. "Can we talk about it at home?"

He smiled at that, the smile that always unraveled her. "Sure."

Later, he poured them each a single malt; the amber liquid caught the light as he handed her the glass. They sank into the couch together, the faint burn of the whisky warming her throat and her courage. He tilted his head at her with that teasing grin. "Do I need to do a drum roll?"

She laughed, but nerves still fluttered inside her. Then she let it out—the fear, the ache, the truth. "When I was talking to Beverly, she told me what that lowlife Walter said happened that night. Michael, it kills me to think—even for a second—that you might believe I encouraged him or flirted with him. That's simply not true. Not even a little. First, I find him repulsive. And second..." Her voice faltered, her chest tightening, but she forced the words out, raw and trembling. "Second, I love you so deeply I could never look at another man the way I look at you."

Michael's expression softened, his smile slow and sure. "I love you, Verónica. And I didn't believe it for one second. I know Walter lied. One day, he'll realize just how big a mistake he made."

A rush of relief flooded her, but the tension didn't ease entirely. "Michael," she whispered, "you're not going to do anything, are you?"

He leaned back, a sly glint in his eyes. "Nothing worth a conversation."

Before she could argue, his arms wrapped around her, his warmth and scent swallowing her whole. He lowered his voice, rough and husky. "Now, let's finish this drink, because I have a rain check to cash."

She pressed against him, her cheek to his chest, holding him tighter than she realized. The relief, the love, the hunger—it all poured into her at once. Her lips brushed his ear as she whispered, "You sure do."

Chapter 27

Verónica

It had been two weeks since that awful night, and Verónica finally felt close to normal again—except for a few dark marks still fading on her face. The swelling was gone, and with her applying just the right amount of makeup, the contusions were hardly noticeable. Michael had insisted she stay home another week, but she needed to get back into the swing of things. She couldn't hide behind closed doors forever. She had been living with him full-time now, barely stopping at her apartment anymore. He told her to give it up, to stop worrying about anything. Yet, for reasons she couldn't fully explain, she hadn't let go of it yet. Maybe it was because what they were sharing sometimes felt too good to be true, like a dream she was afraid might vanish. Still, she needed to reclaim a piece of herself, go into her office, and start feeling like her life was back in some kind of normal rhythm.

Monday morning arrived, and she was ready. Michael had been in the shower at five, gone by six. He drove himself to work because he wanted Grant to drive her around. For now, she agreed. It felt strange at first, but if she was honest, it was also an amazing feeling—to have someone waiting for her outside the building, ready to take her anywhere she needed to go. It was a kind of protection she had never known, and though it felt surreal, she secretly loved it.

When she walked into her office, everyone greeted her warmly, their smiles and kind words wrapping around her like a welcome-back hug. Caroline was the first to run up to her to hug her. Followed by many others in the office. Verónica always felt she was very well-liked in the office, and this reception proved it.

Peter came by not long after. "It's great to have you back," he said, standing in the doorway with practiced sympathy. "I'm so sorry about what happened with Walter. We thought it best that he not return to this office. He's asked me to arrange his transfer to our Tampa office. He apologized profusely and blamed it on the alcohol. Said he never meant to hurt you."

Verónica just stared at Peter, her silence sharp. He shifted uncomfortably and finally said, "Alright then. I'll let you get back to work." She couldn't believe it—that he would even consider helping Walter after what he had done.

Around eleven, her phone lit up with Michael's name. Her heart skipped a beat before she even answered. "Do you have time for lunch?" he asked.

"Yes," she said, perhaps too quickly. As crazy as it sounded, she couldn't wait to see him. She used to go weeks without hearing from him, sometimes months without being in the same room. Now she couldn't get through a single day without craving him.

At lunch, she told him what Peter had said about Walter. The moment the words left her mouth, she saw it—the news hit him like a physical strike. Michael's posture didn't change, but his breathing shifted into something shallow and audible, a dry rasp at the back of his throat. Then came his tell: the slight, unconscious flare of his nostrils, like a hunter catching a scent.

"You mean he didn't fire that piece of shit?" He clipped his words, biting them off at the ends.

He went quiet, his gaze fixed on a point somewhere over her shoulder, his fingers tracing the rim of his water glass. Then he changed the subject; the transition was too fast, too forced. She let it go, though she knew better than to think he had.

Later that afternoon, around two-thirty, Peter appeared at her office again, pale and jittery. "Is everything okay, Verónica?"

"Yes, why?" she asked, puzzled.

"Michael just called and told me to be in his office within the hour. Then he hung up. I have no idea what this is about." His voice trembled with unease.

She fought the urge to smile. "Best you go then," she said gently. The moment he left, she called Michael.

He answered on the first ring. "Hi, baby."

"I miss you already," she whispered, then added, "but that's not why I called. What did you say to Peter? He looks like someone walking toward disaster with no way to stop it."

Michael's laugh rolled through the phone, deep and unrestrained. "Good. That's exactly how I want him to feel."

"Michael…" she cried, her voice teasing, though her heart warmed at his protectiveness.

"Don't worry," he said. "I'll tell you tonight."

"Go easy on him," she whispered. "I know it's personal, but Peter has always treated me kindly—at least since I landed Stratus Meridian Group."

They both laughed, the sound of it easing the edge of the day.

That night, Michael recounted what happened in his office. Verónica listened, mesmerized, as he described Peter walking in to find Ralph and María already waiting like a silent jury. Michael said he hadn't wasted a second, his voice sharp as steel as he repeated the ultimatum he'd delivered.

"I looked him in the eye," Michael said, jaw tight. "I told him, 'I'm saying this once, Peter. You haven't fired that scumbag Walter Brennan yet, and now you're setting him up in Tampa. After what he did to Verónica? Here's the deal: either he's gone—fired without severance—by Friday, or Stratus Meridian Group is no longer your client. I'll pull every contract and make sure every builder in Florida knows how you handle employees who prey on women. Then see how many clients you have left by year's end. Am I clear?'"

Michael said the room went silent. No one dared breathe until Peter finally muttered, "I understand."

"Good," Michael told them. "Then this meeting is over."

When Peter returned to the office later that day, he looked like a man who had been raked over the coals. He didn't speak to Verónica, but by Thursday, a company-wide memo went out. Walter Brennan had been terminated for cause. Delgado, Mercer & Klein, it read, would never tolerate the mistreatment of women by employees or clients.

Verónica smiled to herself as she read it. Warmth spread across her body. She knew without a doubt—Michael was in her corner.

The following week, her cell phone rang. A No Caller ID flashed across the screen. Normally, she would never answer such calls, but something inside her urged her to pick up. Her thumb hovered, hesitated, then pressed accept. Before speaking, she quickly tapped the record button, just in case.

"Hello?" Her voice wavered.

The sound that came next froze her to the core. Walter Brennan.

"You listen to me, you slut," he spat, venom dripping with every word. "You think you can fuck up my life and walk away without consequences? Start looking over your shoulder, bitch. Next time, I'll rip those panties off myself and show you how it feels to be fucked by a real man."

The line went dead.

The phone slipped from her fingers. Her entire body shook as though the venom of his words had poisoned her veins. For a moment, she couldn't breathe. She wrapped her arms around herself, trying to hold together the pieces of her trembling body. Tears burned her eyes, but fear kept them trapped inside. Only one thought cut through the chaos—she needed Michael.

With shaking hands, she dialed his number. He answered in his usual warm, steady tone.

"Hey, baby—"

"Michael..." Her voice cracked, breaking apart. "I'm scared."

The cheer in his tone vanished instantly. "What happened?" His voice was sharp now, commanding.

"I—I just got a call. A terrible call. Can I come to your office?"

"Of course. Stay exactly where you are. Don't move. I'll have Grant at your office in fifteen minutes. Do not leave until he comes up for you. Do you hear me?"

"Yes," she whispered. "I'm so sorry—"

"Don't apologize. Just stay put."

Within fifteen minutes, the reception desk called. "There's a Grant here for you."

She gathered her things with trembling hands and stepped out to meet him. Grant's tall, solid frame filled the doorway. He looked her over in an instant, his sharp gaze taking in her trembling hands and the paleness of her face.

"Ms. Verónica," he said firmly, "are you all right?"

She shook her head, clutching her bag like a shield. "I'm... I'm scared, Grant. I think someone is after me."

He squared his broad shoulders, voice steady as steel. "Don't you worry. No one gets to you without going through me first."

His words settled into her like a fragile thread of comfort. She nodded, following him to the car. He drove her in silence, watchful, steady. When they reached Stratus Meridian Group, they parked in the basement and took the private elevator straight to Michael's floor.

Her legs nearly buckled when she stepped out. At Sara's desk, she asked, "Is he in?" Her voice was barely above a whisper.

Sara gave her a look of quiet concern. "Verónica, yes. Of course. Let me announce you."

The moment Michael's door opened, she couldn't hold herself back. She rushed past Sara and into his arms. The tremors in her body gave her away as she buried herself against his chest. He rose immediately, holding her tight, grounding her.

"Thank you, Sara," he said without looking away from her. Then, softly but urgently, "What happened?"

Still trembling, she sank onto his lap as if it were the only safe place left in the world. Her fingers fumbled with her phone as she pulled up the recording. When she found it, she hit play.

The voice filled the office, venom and filth all over again. She watched Michael's face transform—calmness shattering into a fury she had never seen in him before. His jaw hardened, eyes narrowing to dangerous slits.

He slammed the intercom. "Sara, send Grant in. Now."

She forwarded the recording to him. He played it again, this time with Grant standing in the doorway. Even Grant's expression shifted, storm clouds gathering behind his eyes.

"Get security with you immediately," Michael barked. "Round-the-clock detail. No excuses."

Grant nodded once. "Understood."

Michael turned back to her, his voice softening but still charged with command. "You're going home with Grant. Security will be with you every second. I'll be home later."

She must have looked petrified because his gaze softened further, his hand resting gently against her cheek. He looked at her with such conviction that she found herself finally starting to believe him. "Trust me, Verónica. I will never let anything happen to you."

"Trust me, Verónica. I will never let anything happen to you."

The weight of his words anchored her. She gave him a fragile smile, pressed a trembling kiss to his lips, and let Grant guide her away.

Chapter 28
Michael

As soon as Grant dropped Verónica off, Michael pulled out his cell phone and dialed Vincent. His brother answered on the second ring.

"How's my big brother?" Michael asked casually, keeping his tone light. "Are you free for a drink?"

Vincent chuckled, catching on instantly. He knew this was a conversation that had to be held in private. "Sure, what time?"

"Half an hour." "That'll be fine. Let's go to your favorite place." Michael smiled. Osteria del Mar wasn't his favorite—it was Vincent's.

Michael knew better than to talk on the phone about something like this. It was personal, and he understood the high probability that Vincent's line could be tapped. Both brothers knew the game too well.

Vincent still carried the shadow of the New York mafia family their father had once walked away from. His life, his dealings, the quiet but dangerous web he remained tied to—none of it was ever discussed outside the family. Such conversations didn't belong in public places, not even behind closed doors.

Vincent occasionally assisted Michael with massive construction projects, smoothing union negotiations and ensuring cooperation. The Marino brothers were close, bound by loyalty as much as blood, but Michael, the youngest, had always shared the deepest bond with each of his siblings.

Osteria del Mar was quiet at lunch, the perfect setting. Vincent arrived with two of his men, who stationed themselves at the door. The brothers embraced before settling at a table in the center of the dining room—a deliberate choice to make eavesdropping more difficult. Vincent studied him closely, sharp eyes reading every flicker of expression.

"What's up, Michael?"

Without answering, Michael slid a pair of wired headphones across the table, plugged them into his phone, and hit play. Verónica's recording spilled into Vincent's ears. His expression hardened, and Michael recognized it instantly. That look meant trouble.

"I'll handle it," Vincent said.

"No," Michael cut in. "I want to look him in the eye myself."

"Michael…" Vincent tried to dissuade him, but Michael didn't budge. Finally, Vincent shook his head. "Alright. What's his name?"

"Walter Brennan."

Vincent's brow rose. "Related to Declan Brennan?"

"His brother."

Vincent nodded slowly. "Okay. Give me some time to clear this."

"Thank you."

He leaned back, then smirked. "So when are you marrying this girl you're so in love with?"

Michael smiled despite himself. "Haven't thought about it."

"Don't wait too long. I've seen you with a hundred girls, Michael. But never like this."

Michael laughed softly. "That's what Beverly told me."

"Well, she always knows. Just like Mom."

"That's for sure."

When Michael got home, Verónica was curled on the couch, listening to Whitney Houston. She didn't rise when he walked in, just opened her arms. He sat beside her, and she pressed herself against him, trembling.

"Michael, I'm so scared," she whispered.

"There's nothing to be scared about. He's just a low-life drunk. You've got security all around you. Nothing's going to happen—I promise."

She nodded, but Michael could sense her mind racing elsewhere. Later, when they made love, she gave herself to him, but something was different. She wasn't fully there. For the first time, her fear overshadowed her passion. She tried to satisfy him, and though she did, what burned him was his failure to fully satisfy her. That was when he knew what gave him genuine pleasure. This was a deep love he had never known. Because no other time in his life had a woman's unspoken pain weighed heavier than his own sexual pleasure.

Friday afternoon, Vincent called Michael's office line. "Check your email. Meet me in an hour." His tone was flat, businesslike. Michael told Sara to cancel his four o'clock meeting and left.

The address led him to an abandoned warehouse in a rough part of Miami. Grant parked, and Michael told him, "Stay with the car. I'll be out soon." Inside, he found Vincent. To his right, Walter sat strapped to a chair, flanked by Vincent's men. His face was pale, fear already leaking through the bravado.

"Michael, I was drunk. I meant nothing by it," Walter stammered. "You know I'd never—"

"Cut him loose," Michael said.

Vincent gave a nod, and his men unstrapped him. Walter stood, rubbing his wrists, trying to play defiant.

Michael stepped closer, locking eyes with him. "You will never touch her—or any other woman—again."

And then he let loose. His fists rained down on Walter, each strike fueled by the image of Verónica's tears, her fear, her trembling voice. Blood spattered across Michael's shirt; his knuckles hurt. For a moment, he thought his knuckles might be broken, but he didn't stop. Not until Vincent's men dragged him back.

"I think he's had enough," Vincent said, his voice calm. Walter lay in a pool of his own blood, groaning, broken but alive.

Vincent's gaze was steady on Michael. "Declan cleared this. Walter leaves the state once he has recovered. If he comes back to Florida, he'll never be seen again."

Michael nodded, chest heaving. "Thank you."

"Always," Vincent said.

Outside, Grant saw the blood on him but didn't ask. Michael stripped off his shirt and pulled on his jacket. "Find me a men's boutique in South Beach. White dress shirt, size forty-six long." Grant returned with the shirt, and he changed in the car. His pants were stained, but the black suit masked most of it. At home, he threw everything into the washer—shirt, pants, even his Brioni shoes. Extra soap, long cycle. Then he showered, put on another black suit, an identical tie, and new shoes. Grant bagged the evidence. "Burn it. Then pick up Verónica and take her home," Michael instructed. He nodded.

Michael trusted Grant with his life. A former Navy SEAL who served fifteen years as an FBI agent, Grant carried himself with the quiet authority of a man who had seen everything and survived it.

When Michael first launched Stratus Meridian Group, he needed someone who could dig beneath the surface before committing to multi-million-dollar commercial properties. Grant had just retired from the Bureau when a longtime police officer friend—someone Michael had known since childhood—recommended him.

From that moment, Grant became Michael's shadow, handling investigations whenever called upon.

As Stratus Meridian Group expanded, Grant's role evolved. He was no longer just the investigator; he became Michael's driver, his protector, and ultimately the bodyguard and fixer that Michael relied on above all others.

A few days later, Miami-Dade detectives came to Verónica's office. They told her about Walter—how he'd been found beaten so badly he was barely recognizable. A broken leg, shattered arm, fractured jaw, cheekbone, nose, and a concussion so severe it was a miracle he was alive. The words left her breathless, a strange mixture of relief and unease tightening her chest. Then came the inevitable question—did she know anything about it?

Verónica's hands went cold, but her voice was steady. "No, I don't know anything." The truth was easy; she hadn't been involved. But her emotions betrayed her. A part of her felt vindicated. Walter deserved it—every brutal strike, every broken bone. He had haunted her long enough, made her feel powerless long enough. Now, someone had returned the pain to him tenfold. She didn't say that aloud, but her eyes must have flickered because one of the detectives gave her a knowing look before softening. They nodded, understanding more than their job required, and left.

That night, over a quiet sushi dinner Michael had picked up on his way home, Verónica told him about their visit. She was careful, but he saw the way her chopsticks lingered, the way her lips trembled around her words. She asked softly but directly, "Do you know anything about what happened to Walter?"

Michael looked at her, face unreadable, voice steady. "No one will ever hurt you and walk away smiling."

Her eyes clung to his, searching, peeling back the mask he fought to keep in place. She knew. She didn't need proof, didn't need confessions. The silence between them screamed louder than words ever could. At last, her lips trembled with happiness as she whispered, "Thank you for being there for me." Her voice cracked on the last word; her heart lay bare in that fragile moment. "I love you."

Michael leaned across the table and kissed her, slow and deep, sealing away the truth that didn't need to be spoken. She didn't press again. She didn't have to. And from that night on, they never mentioned the subject again.

Later that night, Verónica suggested they go to bed early. There was a gleam in her eyes, a spark Michael hadn't seen in days. He smiled, already knowing where this was headed. "What a great idea," he said. They walked into the bedroom, and before he could say more, she pushed him down onto the bed. Her fingers slid into his hair, firm, possessive, pulling his mouth back to hers. The kiss wasn't his anymore—it was hers. Demanding. Hungry. Claiming him the way he had claimed her so many times before. Her tongue tangled with his, bold and relentless, leaving him no room to retreat.

He groaned, relief and desire colliding. "Verónica... you're back. I've missed you these last few weeks."

"Shh." Her whisper was hot against his lips as her hands traveled over his chest, down his torso, memorizing every line of muscle. "No more thinking. No more excuses. You want me. I want you. That's all that matters right now."

Her boldness set him on fire. It was as if he were witnessing something fierce and long-starved, finally breaking free from within her. For once, she wasn't waiting for his lead or checking for his permission; she moved with a raw, undeniable urgency.

Michael felt the change in the way she touched him—her hands and mouth claiming him with a desperate intensity, as if she were finally reaching for something she had been denied for far too long. He could see the transformation in the sharp line of her jaw and the predatory heat in her gaze. She was no longer just responding to him; she was taking exactly what she wanted, and the sheer power of her hunger nearly drove him to his knees.

"Verónica—" he tried again, hands gripping her waist to flip her beneath him, but she silenced him with another kiss. This one was slower, deeper, her tongue teasing. She smiled against his mouth, looking triumphant and savoring the feeling of being in control.

"You think you're in control, Michael Marino," she breathed, nipping at his lower lip, "but right now, you're mine."

Her lips trailed fire as she slid down his chest, her tongue leaving wet heat along his skin. With deliberate slowness, she undid his pants, tugging them down, then stripped away his underwear. His arousal stood hard and ready in her hand. She stroked him, licked him, her mouth hot and relentless as she took him deeper between her lips. Pleasure shot through him, a groan torn from his chest.

"Verónica..." His voice was raw, strained. "I need to taste you."

He pulled her body, guiding them into place, laying her across him in opposite directions. Her mouth never stopped working him as he spread her thighs, tasting her sweetness, her slickness. His tongue found her sweet spot, circling and teasing until her hips moved in rhythm with him. Her moans broke against his skin, muffled as her mouth stilled, her head thrown back.

"Oh my God, Michael..." she gasped, high, trembling. "Don't stop. Please—don't stop."

He forgot everything but her. Her taste. Her scent. The way she writhed beneath his mouth. He gave her everything—lips and tongue, pulling her higher until her body trembled violently. She broke apart, crying out his name, the sound muffled against his leg. Her release rushed over him, a flood of heat and satisfaction.

For a moment, she collapsed, breathless, quivering, her legs weak. Then, slowly, she slid her body off him, her mouth finding him again, working his manhood with the same determination. The sensations built too fast, too sharp.

"Verónica—stop," he groaned, grabbing her hips. "I need to be inside you."

She froze, eyes dark, lips glistening. He laid her on her back, fumbling for the drawer, searching. Empty. "Damn," he muttered. "We're out."

Her eyes burned into his, fierce, desperate. "Then forget it. No barriers. I want you bare, Michael. You can pull out."

Her words undid him. With a growl, he spread her thighs and pressed his tip against her slick entrance. The moment he slid inside her, the world disappeared. Heat. Tightness. The raw, intoxicating sensation of being inside her with nothing between them. His body shuddered as he thrust deeper, harder, every stroke pulling a cry from her lips.

"Harder," she begged, nails digging into his lower back. "Deeper—please, Michael!"

He lifted her hips, driving into her with everything he had. She screamed, ragged and beautiful, as her body clenched and released, soaking him in her pleasure. Another climax ripped through her, shaking her apart. The sight, the feel of her, pushed him over the edge. A guttural groan tore from his throat as he exploded inside her, the pleasure fierce and overwhelming.

And then reality hit. Breath still ragged, he collapsed beside her. "Oh God, Verónica," he whispered. "I forgot... I didn't pull out. You felt so amazing. I just couldn't stop. I'm so sorry."

She turned her face toward him, skin still flushed, eyes soft and glowing. She touched his cheek and whispered, "I felt that too, Michael. It's okay. Just hold me."

So he did. He wrapped her in his arms, holding her against him as they lay there for what felt like an eternity. Both of them were silent.

Both of them lost in the reflection of what had just happened and the consequences that could follow.

Chapter 29

Verónica

Verónica opened her eyes the next morning to the sound of Michael shuffling around, getting ready for the gym. He walked out of the bathroom and caught her gaze. His lips curved into a soft smile as he came to the bed. "I'm sorry I woke you, baby. I was trying to be quiet."

She smiled, her voice husky with sleep. "That's okay. Now I get to kiss you goodbye."

He leaned down, kissed her tenderly, and whispered, "I love you. I'm sorry about what happened last night, but I have to admit...it was truly amazing to feel you like that."

Her heart fluttered as she touched his face. "I wouldn't change a thing."

He left for the gym, and she stayed curled beneath the sheets, replaying the night before over and over in her mind. The memories clung to her, flooding her with warmth—and questions she wasn't ready to answer.

At work, Verónica found herself distracted. She repeatedly read the same line, trying to focus, but each time her mind blurred into thoughts of Michael—his touch, his words, his restraint that somehow made her love him even more. But what if last night changed everything? As she thought about it, she realized she could be fertile—her last period had ended a little over a week ago. What if last night left her pregnant? The thought sent a shiver through her. Would it drive him away? Would it ruin what they were building together? She knew one thing with certainty—she could never end a pregnancy. But Michael never mentioned wanting children. Did he even see that in his future? She pressed a hand to her forehead, forcing herself back to the papers on her desk. Worrying wouldn't solve anything.

Around 11:30, her phone chimed. It was a text from Michael.

> I would love to have lunch with you, but I'm buried. See you tonight. I love you.

Her chest tightened, and a smile spread across her lips. She replied with a heart emoji, feeling that familiar rush of warmth that only he gave her.

That evening, when Michael came home, she was already there. He walked in carrying a CVS bag, looking oddly satisfied. She tilted her head. "What did you buy?"

He set the bag down and opened it with a grin. Inside were boxes—so many boxes—of condoms. "This should hold us for a while."

She forced a smile, teasing, "At least a week or two."

But when he walked into the bedroom to change, sadness swept through her without warning. Her stomach tightened as she stared at the pile of boxes. Deep down, she had been hoping—naively, foolishly—that he would say they didn't need them anymore. That one passionate mistake had changed something for him, too. She knew it wasn't fair to expect that, not so soon. He loved her—she didn't doubt that—but expecting him to want a family already was too much. Still, she couldn't help the ache that lingered as she thought about it.

The next six weeks blurred into a fevered rush of passion. Every night, every stolen moment, Michael and Verónica came together with a hunger that felt impossible to satisfy. They burned through box after box until, one quiet morning, Verónica realized something—she was late. Two weeks had passed since her period was due, and a slow, gnawing dread coiled in her stomach. Her usual cramps never came.

She tried to push the thought aside, telling herself it was just nerves. Stress had thrown her cycle off before—especially during the final months of her divorce from Gregory.

But the weeks kept slipping by, and still no period, no cramps, no sign of anything. Ten weeks had passed since the night Michael made love to her bare, and the silence from her own body was becoming impossible to ignore.

Concern settled into her like a weight. She needed to know. During her lunch break, Verónica walked to the drugstore, her hands trembling as she reached for a pregnancy test, the box rattling faintly in her grip. She walked to the counter to pay, standing behind three people in front of her. The fear building inside her—what would the results show? She paid and hurried back to the office.

In the office bathroom stall, with coworkers coming and going outside, she paid them no mind. Hands trembling, she opened the package and removed the test. She positioned it, barely breathing as she waited, then lifted it to look. Two pink lines appeared. Her knees nearly gave out.

Oh God. I'm pregnant.

Her mind spun. No—this couldn't be right. She ran back to the store and bought another, desperate for a different result. But when she tested again, the same lines stared back at her, undeniable and bold. Her chest rose and fell in sharp bursts. Panic tangled with a flicker of joy she didn't dare trust.

Should she tell Michael right away? Should she wait until a doctor confirms it? By the time the workday ended, she had decided—she couldn't keep this from him. She loved him. They had always been honest with each other. He deserved to know.

That night, she left the office early and asked Grant to drive her to Whole Foods. Her mother's old recipes were open on her laptop as she bustled around the kitchen, preparing one of her mom's chicken dinners, apron tied around her waist. It felt comforting—grounding—something familiar on a day when her entire world had tilted.

Michael walked in, eyes widening at the sight of her at the stove. "Wow. I'm impressed. I didn't know you were a chef." He slipped behind her, arms encircling her waist, his voice lowering into that tone that always melted her. "You look so sexy in that apron. I may have to pull you into the bedroom before dinner."

She turned, kissed him softly, and teased, "Not unless you want burnt chicken. Go get changed. I'll wear the apron to bed later."

He grinned, kissed her again, and disappeared to change.

With the food nearly ready, Michael went to the wine room and returned with a magnificent red Burgundy. He placed two beautiful burgundy wine glasses on the table and filled one, just enough to cover the bottom. As he reached for the second glass, she stopped him, gently shaking her head. "Not for me tonight. My stomach was burning this morning. I'd better give it a day."

He smirked. "You're going to let me drink the whole bottle myself?"

She forced a playful smile. "You better not. I want you awake when I wear my apron to bed later."

He laughed, lifted his glass, and joined her at the table. But as they finished dinner, his sharp eyes lingered on her. He set down his glass, leaned forward, and said quietly, "Something is on your mind—and it's not the apron later, is it?"

She smiled and said, "Yes, there is. Let's go sit on the couch." He took his wineglass, and they settled side by side. His arm slid easily around her shoulders, grounding her with that warmth only he carried. He gave her a soft kiss, then pulled back just enough to murmur, "Let me have it."

She stared into those gorgeous eyes, took a deep, steadying breath, and said, "I think I'm pregnant."

For a heartbeat, silence. Then his eyes widened, steady on hers, searching. "Are you sure?"

"According to the home test, I am," she said softly. "I made an appointment with the doctor on Thursday to verify. They will probably just take a blood test."

He leaned back, exhaled, then smiled—not forced, not uncertain, but real. "Let me know what time. I'm coming with you."

She shook her head lightly. "You don't have to."

"I know," he replied, his voice steady, certain. "But I want to."

Tears pricked her eyes. "I know it's a shock, and we didn't plan it. But...are you upset?"

His lips curved, slow and teasing. "Surprisingly, I'm not. The only upsetting thing is—what are we going to do with all those condoms I bought?"

The laughter bubbled out of her before she could stop it. She leaned forward, kissed him, and whispered against his lips, "I love you."

"I love you too," he said, unwavering.

That night, they made love with a passion neither of them seemed able to contain. It felt endless, like the world had narrowed to just them—his mouth, his hands, his body claiming hers over and over. He kissed her until she was trembling, worshiped every part of her until climax after climax tore through her in waves. He took her bare, nothing between them, and for the first time it felt as though they were one in every sense.

In the morning, sunlight spilling across tangled sheets, Verónica was surprised when Michael stayed beside her, foregoing his usual gym routine to take her out to breakfast instead. Over steaming coffee, he looked at her, thoughtful. "All these years, I knew there was always a chance. If it happened, I figured I'd pay for it to be...terminated." He paused, eyes dark, voice low. "But now, with you, that thought is the furthest thing from my mind."

"Thank God, Michael," she whispered, relief rushing through her. "Because I could never terminate what God has created."

He leaned back, his expression turning serious, as if her words had struck a chord deep inside him. "I never thought of it that way. But now that you have me going to church every Sunday, I feel different about it. Remember the first time I came with you to church? I told you how it felt receiving communion for the first time in forever. I said to myself, maybe God was telling me something."

She smiled, eyes shining, and nodded. "Yes."

"Maybe that's why I feel different about this," he said quietly.

She reached across the table, laced her fingers with his, and gave his hand a firm squeeze. "Maybe."

Chapter 30

Michael

After their breakfast, Michael dropped Verónica off at work. On his way to his office, he called his sister. She answered, and he said, "Are you busy today, sis?" She sounded surprised to hear from him so early when she replied, "Actually, I'm not." He said, "I have a ten o'clock meeting in the office. When I'm done, can I swing by and take you to lunch?" He heard her smile and graciously say, "Sure."

After his meeting, he had Grant drive him to pick up Beverly. They went to a new upscale Japanese-owned restaurant downtown for sushi. His sister was a big sushi fan. They got a table in a corner, out of the way, so they could talk. He began with, "I know everything I tell you is guarded with your lips sealed, but please don't even hint at what I'm going to tell you, because it would hurt Verónica." She looked at him seriously and said, "You better not have betrayed this girl, Michael." He said, "Of course not, are you crazy? I love her—just her. No room for anyone else." She smiled and said, "Okay, good. Go ahead, my lips are sealed."

He said, "We didn't plan it. We're always very careful, but somehow it just happened one night, one time—and Verónica is pregnant." Beverly's eyes widened, a smile spreading across her face, but she remained silent, waiting for him to continue. He said, "I don't know how to explain everything I'm feeling. It's only been ten months since I met her, and now she's pregnant. Bev, I thought I'd be upset, but the fact is there's a part of me that is so proud and happy. I want her to have our baby, and I want us to be a family. I want to marry her, but I'm so afraid it's too fast, and people will think I only married her because she got pregnant. Yes, it might be the reason I'm rushing it, but I know I want to marry her at some point, regardless. You know how it will look. What do you think?”

“I think it is music to my ears. I know you, baby brother—I’ve prayed for this day for you for years. I think you've just said it all. Since when does Michael Marino give a damn what anyone else thinks?”

He said, “You’re right, I don’t give a damn—but I care what Dad, you, Anthony, and Vincent think.”

“Well, I can’t speak for them, but I think it’s a gift from God. What do you think Mom would say if she were here?” she asked.

“If Mom were here, I’d be talking to her,” they both laughed.

“I’m sure you would,” she said. “Mom always had the right answers for us. Let me help you with this,” she began, settling back in her chair. “When I met Nick, I was only twenty. I fell in love fast—faster than I expected.”

Michael smiled faintly. “I remember. Dad kept saying it was just a college romance.”

She laughed softly. “Exactly. And less than a year later, Nick asked me to marry him.”

Michael raised an eyebrow. “And you panicked.”

“I didn’t panic,” she corrected, though her grin betrayed her. “I told him I loved him, but I wanted to wait until I graduated. It felt... responsible.”

“And Mom didn’t think so,” Michael guessed.

She shook her head. “Not even a little. I went home that night and told her everything. She looked at me and said, ‘Why are you waiting?’ I told her I thought I should finish school first, let some time pass.”

Michael leaned forward. “And she gave you one of her speeches.”

“One of her best,” she said warmly. “She told me, ‘You can wait, but time is something you never get back. Do you love him? Truly love him like no other?’ And of course, I said yes. Then she asked if I wanted a family. I said yes again. So she said, ‘Then why wait? Maybe God thinks you’re ready. Maybe that’s why Nick asked now.’”

Michael’s expression softened. “She always had a way of making things simple.”

"She did," she agreed quietly. "I went upstairs, thought about it for an hour, then came back down, kissed her on the cheek, and called Nick. Told him I was ready."

Michael smiled. "And the rest is history."

"A year later, Nicholas was born," she said. "And I never once regretted it. Not finishing school later. Not starting our family young. Nothing."

She met Michael's eyes, her tone gentler now. "Life doesn't always wait for perfect timing. Sometimes the right thing just shows up... and you have to be brave enough to accept it."

Michael looked away for a moment, absorbing her words, the weight of memory and possibility settling between them in comfortable silence.

"See, sis, that's why I came to you first. I want to marry her—I didn't realize it before, but I see it clearly now. I love you, Beverly. You are sometimes Mom reincarnated."

She laughed. They finished lunch, and he dropped her back at her office. As soon as Beverly got out of the car, he told Grant to head downtown. "Let's go to the Diamond District."

He walked into the Seybold Building and took the elevator to the fourth floor. As soon as Avi saw him, he looked up and said in his Israeli accent, "Michael, I'm surprised to see you here. I rarely see you in person unless you are picking up something you ordered." Avi had been instrumental in helping Michael acquire many of the Rolex and Patek Philippe watches in his collection. He said, "Avi, I need a very special diamond. At least three carats. Round, gorgeous color, high quality."

Avi smiled. "I just may have what you're looking for. I received it only last week. Let me check the safe in the back. I'll be right back."

Moments later, he returned, unfolding a black cloth across the counter and laying out four stones, each round and nearly identical in size. Using his jeweler's tweezers, he lifted them one at a time, studying each through his magnifier before finally selecting one.

"This one is exquisite," he said, holding it toward Michael. "Just under four carats. You can see the faint hint of blue in the stone.

Almost flawless—even under the lens. Michael, it's one of the finest stones I've seen. But it isn't inexpensive."

Michael kept his eyes on the diamond. "How much?"

Avi replied, "I would charge anyone else four hundred thousand. Because it's you—and because of the business we've done—I'll give it to you for three twenty-five. Trust me, you won't find a finer stone at a better price."

"Sold," Michael said. "Now let's look at settings."

"White gold, I assume," Avi said.

Michael nodded. He chose a setting and asked, "When will you have it ready?"

"I have the polisher and the setter... how about Friday?"

"Friday morning would be great."

Avi smiled. "It will be ready."

Michael finally felt certain—this was what he wanted.

He went home that night and found Verónica curled up on the couch, her legs tucked beneath her as she read. Her face was calm, almost glowing; the lamp's light painted her in a warm halo. He leaned against the doorway for a moment, just watching her, before asking softly, "What are you reading?"

Without looking up, she held the book slightly higher and said, "A new one by Dr. Emily Hartman—she's a leading pediatrician. How to Feed Yourself to Protect the Health of Your Baby."

His chest tightened with pride and something deeper—an ache he couldn't quite name. He crossed the room, kissed the top of her head, and said, "You're going to be a magnificent mother."

She lowered the book then, her eyes shimmering with that soft, knowing smile that always undid him.

Later that night, they made love. It wasn't just sex anymore—hadn't been for a while. Every time he touched her, kissed her, tasted her, it was love you could touch—warm, with a certainty of connection. He worshiped her body as if it were something holy, refusing to stop until she cried out his name, her voice breaking in a scream that still echoed in him.

With nothing separating them now, their connection felt deeper than ever—skin to skin, soul to soul. He felt her completely, raw and deep, every inch of him inside her. He tried to hold back, to wait for her again, but the intensity was too much. The moment overtook him, and he surrendered, groaning her name against her mouth.

When he collapsed beside her, still trembling, she laughed softly, kissed his jaw, and whispered, "Then we'll just have to do it again."

And they did—an hour later, tangled in sheets and sweat, giving each other over to ecstasy once more.

On Thursday morning, at eleven sharp, he went with Verónica to her doctor's appointment. He'd never felt prouder to be at her side. Sitting there, holding her hand as the doctor examined her, he knew this was more than love, more than lust—it was life, theirs together.

When they finally sat in the doctor's office, Verónica's fingers threaded through his. The doctor smiled and said everything looked good—that she was, without question, pregnant, twelve weeks.

A lump rose in his throat, so thick he could barely swallow. For the first time, he understood how Anthony must have felt when he learned Angela was pregnant. That same mix of disbelief, joy, and a strange, protective fear.

When they left, Grant was waiting outside. He drove them each to work, but the world around him felt different. Bigger. More fragile. More beautiful.

He called Verónica around lunchtime and told her he would pick up sushi for dinner. She immediately stopped him. "Michael, Dr. Hartman says no raw food."

"Oh, okay," he replied. "What do you feel like having?"

"How about Italian tonight? Do you want to go out?"

"Let's stay in," he said. "I'm tired. How about pizza?"

"Perfect," she answered with a soft laugh. Michael smiled to himself, keeping the secret of the unforgettable evening he was planning for her tomorrow at Osteria del Mar.

Friday morning arrived, and he hit the gym at six sharp, needing to burn off nervous energy. Grant took Verónica to work, then swung by the office to pick him up. They headed downtown to the jewelry district, where Avi had the ring waiting. It sparkled inside a blue velvet box, catching the light as if it had been made to capture her soul. His hands trembled as he held it, thinking of the words he would say.

At eleven-thirty, he called her. "Do you still feel like Italian for dinner? I want to take you to Osteria del Mar for dinner tonight," he told her.

Her voice carried a smile, the kind that made his heart skip. "That sounds wonderful. Do I need to know if it's anything special that I need to dress for?"

"No," he said carefully. "I just love you, and I enjoy seeing you all dressed up."

Grant would pick her up at three-thirty from work, giving her time to go home, change, and prepare. He could hear the excitement in her tone, even though she was keeping her words casual. He phoned the restaurant and reserved his favorite corner table, tucked away from the crowd, where the world would shrink down to just them.

They arrived at six o'clock. The maître d' greeted them and led them straight to the corner. Verónica looked radiant, her glow un-deniable, a softness in her features that made him want to freeze the moment. She ordered a Virgin Mary; he ordered a Martini, and they toasted quietly. His throat tightened.

"I have something to ask you," he said, holding her gaze.

Her eyes widened, a smile tugging at her lips. "Of course."

He reached for her hand, steadying himself. "I've thought about this deeply, Verónica. Clearly. Will you marry me?"

Her face lit up, joy spilling from her in waves. "Oh, Michael—I never thought I could be as happy as I am at this moment. Yes. Yes. A thousand times, yes. I love you so much."

He leaned across the table and kissed her, sliding the velvet box from his pocket. He set it before her, watching as her breath caught. She looked at the box and opened it slowly, her eyes shimmering as tears fell.

"Oh my God…it's so gorgeous." Her fingers trembled as she slipped the ring onto her finger. "I will never take it off. Michael, it's the most beautiful ring I've ever seen."

He smiled, heart full, but he wasn't finished. "One more thing."

She blinked, surprised. "What could top this?"

"I don't think we should wait," he said, his voice low and sure. "I want to see you walk down the aisle in a white dress before it becomes obvious you're pregnant. I don't care what anyone thinks or says anymore. But I want this for you—for us. You always dreamed of a church wedding. Let's do it soon. Soon."

She drew a sharp breath; her whole body seemed to be trembling with joy. "Michael... I can't tell you how happy I am right now. You are not going to sleep tonight, Michael Marino, so don't drink too much."

He laughed, already knowing she was right.

Chapter 31

Verónica

The joy Verónica was experiencing was beyond words, a happiness so overwhelming it filled every corner of her being. She had a new bounce in her step, and she felt a radiance in her expression that seemed to mirror the deep, admiring smile on Michael's face. She had a new bounce in her step. Her face had a glow Michael had not seen before, and it made him smile deeply. As soon as they got home, she grabbed her phone and called her sister, her voice trembling with excitement as she told her the news. Donna's reaction was immediate—her laughter and squeals of joy poured through the speaker, wrapping Verónica in her happiness. She heard the excitement in her sister's voice, the pride, the love. "Boy, were you wrong, little sister," Donna teased, reminding her of all the doubts she had whispered over the past months. Verónica smiled through tears and admitted softly, "Isn't that the truth?"

Donna was the only one she had confided in about the pregnancy—just yesterday afternoon, she had called her, unable to keep it to herself any longer. Donna had asked her the hard question she hadn't dared voice aloud: did she think Michael would want to marry her, or was he the type to walk away? Verónica's answer had been simple, steady, and filled with certainty. "No. He would never walk away. I know he loves me. I just didn't know if marriage was even in his vocabulary."

Later, as she stood with Michael in their living room, her hand resting against the small but growing baby in her stomach, she whispered, her voice catching, "I so wish my mother could have been alive to see this joy you've given me. Both in my heart and in my stomach."

His eyes softened, his hand rested gently against her cheek as he smiled with that warmth that made her fall in love all over again. "I know exactly what you mean," he said gently. "My mom would have loved you."

They stood there, wrapped in each other's arms, holding on as though the world outside no longer mattered. Minutes passed—or maybe it was only seconds—but in that embrace, it felt like time itself had stopped. Her chest ached with love, with gratitude, with an ache for all the years she thought she'd never feel this kind of joy. Then, with a rush of boldness surging through her, she pulled back just enough to look at him. Her voice was low, commanding, trembling with both desire and power. "Get in the bedroom," she told him, her eyes locked to his, "and remove every piece of clothing you have on."

Michael's lips curved into a slow, knowing smile, a spark of heat igniting in his gaze. "Yes, ma'am," he murmured, his voice rich with hunger, before turning toward the bedroom. Verónica's heart pounded with anticipation, knowing tonight she would not only give him her love but take control of it.

They lay on the bed, wrapped in each other, lips locked in deep, consuming kisses that stole every ounce of breath from her body. His mouth moved to her neck, each brush of his lips igniting waves of heat down her spine. When she whispered, she wanted to please him first; he pulled back just enough to look into her eyes, his voice rough, commanding, yet tender. "If you want to please me, lie here and let me make you scream. That's what gives me pleasure." The words melted through her, and she smiled at him, unable to hide the way her heart swelled with love.

His hands caressed her breasts, teasing until her nipples tightened beneath his touch. When his mouth closed around them, sucking until they ached, a cry escaped her. She tangled her fingers in his hair, urging him on, trembling as he kissed down her stomach and settled between her legs. The first touch of his tongue against her heat made her arch off the bed, gasping. He moved with slow, deliberate strokes, circling, teasing, savoring every sound he pulled from her. The pressure built, and when he lifted her against his mouth, his tongue pressed firmly to her sweet spot, driving her wild, relentless, and perfect. Her moans turned to desperate cries as the wave crested, and then she shattered, convulsing, trembling, screaming his name as the release tore through her.

Weak, bliss-drunk, she collapsed against the pillows, her body quivering as he climbed back up, gathering her in his arms. His kiss was hungry, claiming, and when she tasted herself on his lips, she felt another rush of heat course through her. He smiled wickedly, his voice low against her mouth. "Now you see why I love pleasing you with my tongue."

That was the moment she knew—she needed to take control of him. Desire surged through her, fierce and consuming. She pushed him back against the bed, straddling his chest, her lips and tongue trailing across the hard planes of his body. His muscles flexed beneath her; his moans deepened when she teased his nipples with her mouth. Her hand slid lower, over his taut stomach, until she wrapped her fingers around the thick length of him, throbbing and hard. The sheer power of his arousal in her hand made her ache to have him inside her.

She stroked him slowly at first, then faster, licking along his shaft before taking him into her mouth. His taste filled her; his groans sent shivers straight to her core. She took him deeper, pushing until he hit the back of her throat, and his body tensed beneath her. When she felt him pulse, on the brink of release, she pulled away with a sly smile, knowing she wanted to feel him fill her.

In one swift movement, he rolled her beneath him, spreading her legs wide. She gasped when his tip pressed against her soaked entrance. He pushed inside, slowly at first, stretching her, filling her, making her body tremble with every inch. The sensation was overwhelming, exquisite. She clung to him, urging him deeper, faster, moving her hips to meet his thrusts. His pace quickened, harder, stronger, until he found that perfect spot that sent lightning through her body. She screamed his name, another climax tearing her apart, shaking her to her core.

Michael gripped her hips, driving deeper until his own release ripped through him with a groan of pure ecstasy. "Oh my God, Verónica... you feel so amazing. I can never get enough of you." He collapsed against her, both of them slick with sweat, hearts pounding in perfect rhythm. She wrapped her arms tightly around him, whispering into his ear with every ounce of truth in her. "Michael, you are everything to me."

He held her tighter still, smiling into her skin as if he never wanted to let her go.

They lay tangled in the sheets, her cheek resting against the steady rise and fall of his chest, when his words nearly stopped her heart. "When should we get married?" he asked. Everything was happening so fast, so impossibly fast, yet it felt as though she had been waiting her entire life for this question. Her lips parted, hesitant. "I'm not sure," she whispered, her mind racing through the chaos of everything that still needed to be done.

He turned his head to study her, eyes soft but unwavering. "Do you want a big wedding?" he asked. She shook her head instantly. "No. I don't care about that. All I want is to be your wife." Yet a flicker of doubt trailed after her words. She said, "You have a big family, endless business associates—surely you would want the grand spectacle to accommodate all of them." But when he smiled, his voice was firm, certain. "Verónica, normally that would be true. There would be fanfare, flashing lights, and endless toasts. But I don't want that anymore. All I want is you. Let's keep it small. Just family. Or—" his lips curved, teasing, "we could make it a destination wedding if you'd like."

She closed her eyes for a moment, her mother's face flooding her thoughts. "I want to marry you here," she said softly, "in the church I used to go to with my mother." The words carried the weight of longing and memory, and when she opened her eyes, he nodded without hesitation. "Then that's where it will be." Her heart swelled, tightening in her chest, as though he had just given her back a piece of her past.

His tone warmed, playful again. "Let's hold the reception at the restaurant in the hotel where we met for Thessaly's wedding. That's where it began, so it's only fitting." She laughed, joy bubbling through her, because it was perfect. "That's a wonderful idea," she said, her pulse fluttering as she imagined it.

Michael nodded, his eyes sparkling as he leaned in closer. "I'll have Sara call to arrange the restaurant for the day and evening. Now, the only question is—what day?"

Her stomach tightened, nerves and excitement colliding. "Two months?" she suggested cautiously. But he grinned, shaking his head. "I was going to say one month." Her laughter spilled out before she could stop it, the sound giddy and breathless. "So let's compromise," he continued. "Six weeks."

She kissed him softly, the taste of forever on her lips. "I love you," she whispered, her chest tight with gratitude, disbelief, and desire all at once. "Okay—six weeks from this Saturday. We'll need to check with the church." His brows lifted, a playful challenge glinting in his eyes. "Do you want to handle that, or should I have Sara do it?"

She sat up slightly, brushing his cheek with her fingers; her decision was clear. "No. Let me handle it. This one's mine."

Chapter 32

Verónica

Monday, Verónica sat in her office, pretending to work but failing miserably. Her mind wasn't on contracts or deadlines—it was lost in the cloud she'd been floating on since Friday night. The documents blurred before her until she finally set them down and reached for the phone. She needed to tell someone, someone who would understand. She called Thessaly.

She answered cheerfully, "Where have you been hiding?"

Verónica laughed, her heart racing. "So many things are happening so fast. Let me start with this—I have a gorgeous, magnificent diamond ring on my finger."

She screamed so loud that Verónica had to pull the phone from her ear. "Oh my God, that's amazing! Who? When? You didn't even tell me you were seeing someone!"

"I know," Verónica said, grinning so wide her cheeks ached. "Are you sitting down?"

"I am now. You have my full, undivided attention."

"The man I'm so deeply in love with… You already know him."

There was silence, then a squeal. "My cousin, Michael?"

"Yes," Verónica said, laughing.

"I knew you disappeared with him at my wedding, but I never thought—oh my God, that's incredible! Verónica, I never thought Michael would settle down. You know my cousin is gorgeous? And rich?"

Verónica pressed the ring against her chest, her heart swelling. "Yes, he's gorgeous. I know. But he's so much more than that, Thessaly. He fills my heart in ways I never imagined. He makes me whole."

"I'm so happy for you, Verónica. So happy for both of you. When's the wedding?"

She bit her lip, savoring the moment. "Well... there's more."

"Do tell."

"I'm not only getting married. We're having a baby. I'm pregnant."

There was a sharp gasp, then more squealing. "Oh my God! That's wonderful!"

Then Thessaly lowered her voice. "Okay, I'm not supposed to say anything yet, but I don't care. I didn't even tell my mother yet—I'm pregnant too. We can raise our babies together!"

They both exploded with laughter and shrieks of joy. "How far along are you?" Verónica asked.

"Eleven weeks."

Verónica pressed a hand to her stomach. "Oh my God. I'm twelve weeks. Can you believe this? We're going to go through it together. Now, when it gets hard, we'll have each other to cry on."

They laughed again; the excitement was overwhelming.

"So back to the wedding," Verónica said breathlessly. "Michael wanted it in a month, I thought two months, so we agreed on six weeks. That makes it Saturday, January 12th."

"I'm circling my calendar right now," Thessaly said.

"I have to call Susan next," Verónica told her.

Thessaly giggled. "Don't tell me she's pregnant too."

"No way," Verónica laughed. "But I'll let you know when everyone knows. Michael probably wants to make it official himself, so don't tell anyone else yet."

"Girl, it's going to be so hard to keep my mouth shut, but for you, I'll do it. Just give me the green light when it's time to broadcast."

Verónica laughed, her chest so full she thought she'd burst. "I will."

After they hung up, Verónica called Susan, but got her voicemail. She left a message for her to call back.

Then she sat down to make a wedding list. Donna would be her maid of honor—of course. That made five people. Thessaly and her husband. Susan and whoever she brought. If Michael wasn't inviting anyone from work, maybe she shouldn't either, but Caroline had become a dear friend, and she wanted her there.

She picked up her phone and called Michael. "Hi, baby," he said, his voice warm. "How's your day?"

"Wonderful," Verónica said, almost breathless. "You have me floating on a cloud. I started making a list for the wedding, and I wanted to ask if you're planning to invite anyone from the office."

"Let's discuss tonight," he said smoothly. "I have a few people in my office for a meeting right now."

She blushed, even though he couldn't see her. "I'm so sorry. Why didn't you say something?"

"Because I'm the boss," he said, his voice low and sure, "and you come first."

Her smile was so wide it hurt. "I love you."

"I love you too."

"Talk later," she whispered and hung up, still glowing, still dizzy with bliss.

Later that night at dinner, they spread the notepad across the table, the air between them charged with anticipation as they began discussing the wedding and who to invite. Michael rattled off names while Verónica scribbled them down quickly, trying to keep pace. When he finally leaned back, she glanced at the list and froze. "Michael, do you know how many people this is?" she asked, staring at the page in disbelief. He shook his head with a casual shrug, looking completely unbothered by the growing list. "No, but I figured maybe around fifty." She swallowed a laugh, more stunned than amused. "Over a hundred and twenty already—and that's without even counting all the people you deal with outside the office. There's no way a restaurant can handle that."

He frowned, his brow creasing as he pushed his glass aside. "What are we doing?" he asked quietly. "We said we wanted a small, private wedding." His voice softened, almost pleading, as if the thought of something simple mattered more to him than the grandeur others might expect.

She pulled the pad closer and drew a line across the page, starting fresh. "All right. Just immediate families," she said firmly, and began again. She did the math as she wrote: nine for his family, five for hers. She couldn't imagine it without Thessaly and her husband, and of course, Susan, who would insist on bringing a date. Michael nodded, agreeing, then added, "Sara and her husband. No one else from the office. If I invite one, I'll have to invite them all."

She looked down at the new total—thirty-five. Only thirty-five. The number made her breathe easier, as if the weight of obligation had suddenly lifted. "That's it," she whispered, smiling softly.

Michael's lips curved in a grin, relief flashing in his eyes. "Then let's plan on the restaurant again," he said. His hand covered hers on the table, and in that moment, it felt right—intimate, theirs, exactly as they wanted it.

Michael said, "I have something else to discuss with you." Verónica looked at him and wondered what he was thinking now. He said, "Do you think it's time you gave up your apartment?" She smiled and said, "Yes. I have been living with you for a few months now, sharing your closet, and it finally feels real. I will take care of that tomorrow." Michael smiled and said, "About you sharing my closet. You're right—it is my closet, and I don't think that's the way we want to start this marriage. So I decided, as much as I love this penthouse, it is one I designed and built with other people's style and input. I want us to have something we both want, build, and design. What do you think of us moving into the penthouse at Solara Edge when it's completed? We are ready to select all the finishes. You can design the whole thing. You can work with the design team and make everything just the way you want it."

Her eyes welled up, and she said, "Michael, you never stop amazing me. I would love to do that with you. Then it can be ours." He smiled and said, "I will instruct the design team to call you and set up whatever time you have free to start the process."

Verónica watched Michael over the rim of her glass, sensing the shift in the air before he even spoke. He leaned back, his usual poise replaced by a restless energy she hadn't seen in him before.

"The last thing we have to discuss is the uncomfortable subject of the prenup," Michael said, offering a small, self-deprecating chuckle. "You know how lawyers are. They live to imagine every worst-case scenario."

She caught the slight tension in his shoulders and the way he wouldn't quite meet her gaze. It was a fascinating tell. Here was a man who had spent his entire life across boardroom tables, shark-like and unyielding, negotiating multi-million dollar contracts without breaking a sweat. Yet, discussing a financial safety net with her clearly made him feel like he was treading on glass.

Verónica reached across the table, her smile soft and reassuring. "I knew that was coming, Michael. Any lawyer worth their salt would insist on one, especially with everything you've built. Honestly, I'd be worried about their competence if they didn't."

She squeezed his hand, wanting him to feel the sincerity behind her words. "I'm perfectly fine with a prenup. I'm not here for the empire or the bank accounts. I just want you. I want our baby. What you've built belongs to you, and I don't want or expect any of it. I want this to be nothing more than a stack of paper that we sign and never have to look at again."

Michael didn't wait for her to finish before he was leaning forward, his hand tightening around hers. "Verónica, listen to me."

His voice dropped an octave, vibrating with an intensity that made her heart skip. "You've shown me more love than I ever thought I was capable of receiving. You've changed everything for me. No matter what the future holds, I need to know—deep in my soul—that you and the baby will never want for a single thing. I'm going to make sure this document takes care of you both for the rest of your lives. That's non-negotiable."

The raw protectiveness in his tone brought a sting of tears to her eyes. She saw the sincerity in the dark depths of his gaze, a promise that went far beyond legal clauses and signatures. She realized then that for Michael, this wasn't about guarding his wealth from her; it was about using that wealth to build a fortress around her.

She gave him a slow, trusting nod. "Whatever the lawyers write up, Michael—if you agree to it, I'll sign it. I trust you."

He let out a long, ragged exhale, as if a massive weight had finally been lifted from his chest. He reached up, cupping her cheek with a hand that was uncharacteristically trembling.

"I love you, Verónica," he whispered, the words carrying more weight than any contract they would ever sign.

Chapter 33

Michael

The next six weeks flew by, with so much to do to prepare for the wedding. Verónica worked closely with Sara to finalize arrangements with the church and the restaurant. At the same time, she became deeply involved with the design team, so much so that she rarely had time for lunch. Strangely, the long hours didn't seem like a burden to her—she had a vibrant energy he hadn't seen before, as if the project were fueling her rather than draining her. The penthouse drawings looked incredible, and for the first time, Michael could see that she felt she was contributing and building something uniquely hers.

One day, Michael called Barbara into his office. She was the manager of the design team assigned to the Solara Edge project. He asked how things were going. She seemed almost surprised by the question, given how much Verónica had already been involved. Barbara said things were going great, then leaned in and added, "Honestly, between you and me, Verónica is a natural at design. I've been so impressed with her sense of style and color coordination. She has a genuine talent. I originally thought she'd just ask for suggestions or pick from a few samples. But she knew exactly what she wanted. After I saw the whole concept she put together, I was blown away." Barbara smiled and added with a laugh, "She's in the wrong business."

He watched her from across the table. She pushed her food around, lost in thought. When she finally looked up, her eyes were steady but carried a quiet heaviness.

"I've been thinking about leaving Delgado," she said.

Michael froze and remained silent.

"I want to focus on the baby. And on our new place," she said. She looked down at her hands. "But it feels strange to think about not working. After my divorce, this job helped me find myself again, and then it brought me to you. The idea of leaving it is a little scary."

Michael smiled. He had expected this. "Come to Stratus. Barbara keeps talking about your eye for design. She says you have a gift."

Verónica's face lit up. "That's sweet of her. I'm actually starting to love it." She leaned in, her eyes playful. "You just want me in your office, on your couch, whenever you want."

He laughed, surprised. "I hadn't thought of that, but now that you mention it, I love the idea."

Her smile softened. She studied his face, searching for any catch. "You'd really want me around all the time?"

"Every second," he said, and he meant it.

"Okay. But Michael, only until the baby is born. I want to raise our child the way our mothers raised us."

Her eyes shimmered with a mix of warmth and old-fashioned resolve.

Michael nodded, understanding. "Stratus is growing. We now have three design teams, and more are coming. I need someone to coordinate everything and report to me. You could help until I find someone permanent."

He watched her think it over. He could see the professional and the soon-to-be mother struggling inside her.

"Think about it," he said quietly. "Let me know."

Michael had spent the week watching the quiet resolve settle over Verónica. He didn't press her; he knew the weight of the choice she was making. But when he walked into the apartment that Monday evening, the tension in her shoulders had vanished, replaced by a radiant, unmistakable sense of relief.

"It's done," she said, sinking into the leather chair in the living room.

Michael sat across from her, studying the triumphant spark in her eyes. "How did Peter take it?"

"He looked stricken at first," she said, a small, wry smile tugging at her lips. "I think he saw his biggest account—your account—walking out the door with me. He actually looked like he was bordering on a panic attack."

Michael felt a flicker of grim satisfaction. He knew how the game was played and exactly how much Peter relied on the Stratus account. "And you gave him the news?"

"I did." She nodded, her expression softening. "I told him exactly what you said—that the account would stay with Delgado, Mercer & Klein and that he would be the primary contact from now on. You should have seen him, Michael. It was like watching a man receive a stay of execution. He was so relieved, he would have agreed to anything I asked for."

Michael watched her as she spoke, noting the way her hands were finally still, no longer fidgeting with her rings. He'd given her the leverage she needed to walk away on her own terms, and seeing her this empowered was priceless.

Her last day at Delgado, Mercer & Klein was that Friday. Monday morning, Michael arrived at the office to find her already settled into the space Sara had prepared for her. He paused at her door, noticing her head down as she reviewed design plans, a soft humming drifting into the hallway. This was more than a new challenge—it was a new chapter, one that tied her future more deeply to Michael's.

The weeks flew by, and Saturday, January 12th, was upon them. It was the Friday night before the wedding. Verónica and Michael ordered Chinese food for dinner. After dinner, they sat in the living room listening to music while Michael sipped a single malt. Michael said, "I guess it's time for me to go." She replied, "I'm sorry you have to leave your apartment." He smiled and said, "It's perfectly fine, but let's not make a habit of this. The comfort of your warm body next to me as I sleep and wake is something I've become accustomed to." Michael was going to Anthony's house so Verónica could have the entire apartment to get dressed in her white wedding dress the following day. Thessaly and Susan were coming over in the morning to help her, along with a makeup artist and beautician.

It was 10:00 pm when Michael stood and said, "I'll see you tomorrow at the church." She whispered, "You have no idea how hard it is for me not to pull you into that bedroom and rip your clothes off." He answered, "Yes, I do—as evidenced by my not having you spread out on the bed right now without a stitch of clothing." They hugged and kissed for a few minutes, and then, before he lost control, Michael said, "I have to go." She smiled and said, "I love you." "I love you too, baby," he replied.

Anthony, Michael's brother, partner, and best man, arrived at the church at 12:30 pm. The wedding was at 1:00 pm. On the way, Anthony told Michael how happy he was for him. He knew this was the right thing and that they would once again be one happy family—albeit bigger, with a few extra little ones running around for Sunday dinners.

When the limo pulled into the church parking lot, Michael leaned forward, his brow furrowing as he glanced at the sea of cars stretching across the rows. "Why are there so many cars here? Is something else going on?" he asked Anthony, his tone edged with genuine surprise.

Anthony looked out the window, wearing a perplexed expression. "No clue, brother," he replied, shaking his head as if just as baffled.

They stepped out of the limo, the beautiful sunlight brushing against their suits as the sound of distant chatter drifted from the church steps. Michael's curiosity turned to astonishment the moment they entered. The church was filled; every pew occupied, the air alive with anticipation.

He followed Anthony down a narrow side hallway toward the front, but when Michael stepped out and truly saw the crowd, the breath caught in his throat. Familiar faces filled the church—employees who had stood by him through late nights and long deals, vendors who had worked alongside him on projects, distant relatives he hadn't seen in years, and friends who had been part of his journey. It felt as though every thread of his life had woven itself into this moment, gathered under one roof.

Leaning slightly toward Anthony, he whispered with a half-smile, "Maybe we should have had a huge wedding."

Anthony chuckled, his hand patting Michael's shoulder with brotherly reassurance. "What you're doing is fine. There wasn't enough time for a huge wedding anyway."

Michael's chest tightened with unexpected emotion. He hadn't expected this—so many people, uninvited to the reception, showing up simply to witness the moment that mattered most. The church was full of magnificent flower arrangements throughout. The sound of so many people chatting and waiting—the organist played softly in the background. He felt honored, humbled, and deeply touched that they had come not for the celebration afterward, but for the sacred vows he was about to make. It was as if the entire community had gathered to bless his union, and the weight of that love filled him with a profound sense of gratitude.

The sudden fanfare of the horns echoed through the sanctuary, and Michael felt a jolt of pure anticipation. He knew the signal—the white Rolls-Royce had just pulled up to the curb outside. From his place at the altar beside Anthony, he watched the heavy doors at the back of the church swing open, and his breath caught. Michael's father, Dominic, appeared in the doorway, beginning the slow walk to lead Verónica down the aisle. Michael had expected her to ask her brother-in-law to give her away, but he was pleasantly surprised she felt close enough to his father to ask him instead. Dominic looked as proud as Michael had ever seen him.

Michael watched her walking down the aisle; the glow on her face, the excitement in her eyes, was beyond words. He was so proud and happy to be the one waiting for her at the steps of the altar. She looked exquisite—ready for a wedding magazine shoot. The ceremony and the Mass were beautiful. The priest was wonderful.

As they left the church arm in arm, Michael was finally married to a woman he truly wanted to spend the rest of his life with. She filled his cup in every imaginable way. God had truly blessed him.

Chapter 34

Epilogue

Verónica had been married to the love of her life for seven months now. Her baby was growing inside her, and she was so excited to see him when he was born. Yes, it was a he. She and Michael had decided two months ago, when the doctor asked if they wanted to know, that they did. Verónica could still see the absolute ecstasy that had transformed Michael's face the moment the doctor told them it was a boy. Now they were talking about names. She wanted to name him Michael after his father, but Michael thought they should name him Dominic after his grandfather.

Michael had been so attentive and loving during her pregnancy. He fulfilled her in so many ways. She had heard from many of her friends—even her sister—that as the pregnancy progressed, men tended not to be as interested in sex. She hadn't noticed that one bit with Michael. He held her and wanted her as much as he always had. Her big belly limited her in positions, but her satisfaction hadn't been hindered in the least. She loved feeling his skin against hers, the feel of his lips when he kissed her, the feel of his body when he made love to her. Her climaxes were still incredible and sometimes even more intense.

It was Sunday late morning, two weeks before her due date, and they were getting ready to go to Michael's father's for Sunday dinner. She was moving pretty slowly, carrying 32 pounds more. She was sitting on the bed when Michael walked out of the bathroom wearing nothing but his underwear. She looked at him and smiled. "I know we have to go, but come sit with me."

He smiled and did so.

"You look so sexy, you're making me horny," she whispered.

He smiled again, took her hand, and kissed her gently on the lips.

"You know it's been two weeks since we made love," she said softly. "I know the doctor said it would be better for me not to have intercourse or external manipulation, but she didn't say anything about me pleasing you."

She leaned in to kiss him, sliding her hand below his stomach and under his underwear. She immediately felt his manhood harden against her touch.

"I'm always horny when I'm with you," he murmured. "I get incredible sexual fulfillment when I'm able to please you—I can wait."

"But I can't," she breathed. "I want you now."

She pushed him onto the bed and continued to feel his excitement. His moans made her feel alive, powerful, and adored. As she licked his length and stroked him, his body trembled, his voice deep with pleasure. She slid her mouth over his tip and slowly enjoyed every inch of him. When she sucked harder, she felt him throb. She knew it had been two weeks for him, so this wouldn't take long.

"Oh God, Verónica, you feel amazing," he groaned. "I feel like it's been forever."

She took him deeper, faster, until he cried out, exploding in her mouth. She wanted every drop of him, wanted him to feel completely undone by her. His release filled her with a satisfaction she couldn't put into words.

"Verónica," he said breathlessly, his hand in her hair, his eyes burning into hers. "You make me feel amazing. I love you—like I never thought I could love another."

Those words alone filled her heart with joy, spreading through every corner of her body.

When they got home later that night, she was tired. Her head rested on the pillow as she lay on the bed, her hand naturally settling on her stomach, feeling a kick of the life to come. The thought of being a mother filled her with trembling anticipation, both beautiful and terrifying. She closed her eyes and imagined what it would feel like to cradle their child in her arms—hoping he had Michael's eyes, his strength, his love, his passion. The idea consumed her with wonder, her heart swelling until she thought it might burst.

Michael came and lay beside her, his touch slow, reverent, as though he already understood the weight of what she was dreaming of. When his hand covered hers, resting gently against her stomach, her entire being melted. No man had ever made her feel this way—not just desired, but adored, chosen, safe. Every whisper of his breath against her skin reminded her she was no longer alone in the world.

She opened her eyes and looked at him, really looked at the intensity in his gaze, at the unspoken vow he gave her every time he touched her. In that moment, she knew she had never been more cherished. She was not just Verónica; she was the attorney fighting for a place in a man's world. She was his woman; she could see it in the depth of his gaze—that she was the one who truly stirred his soul, the one who, God willing, would soon give birth to his child.

Want More?